PHANTASMAGORIA

A Collection of Short Stories

By Nicole Mello

This book is dedicated to women, queers, the oppressed, and the outcasts. This world is ours. Let's take it back.

PREFACE

This book was a long time coming. A lot of the stories I've written have been tremendously long undertakings. If you've read *Venus* or *The Modern Prometheus,* you know just how loquacious I can be. I have a lot to say. The thing is, the books I've published before have been novels: massive undertakings that tell a larger story. This book is not that.

What you have in your hands is a collection of short stories. I wrote each of these stories for myself. This is the first time I have ever done something like that. Each one is unique in that each one features me working my way through something in my own life, or in my own world, or in my own brain. What does it mean to die? What does it mean to live? Why must we suffer? How do we stop our own suffering? They're big questions, and I use vampires and serial killers and bacchanalias to answer them.

This is a collection of dark comedies. Each story is both humorous and heinous. Humor is our greatest weapon. Use it even in the worst of times. I highly recommend it. These stories are united by their humor and their comedic value, as well as by how dark and horrendous they can be within that humor. There's so much bad, but if we can laugh at it, it's a little bit better. If laughing at it isn't for you, give it a shot anyways. You might find something you like; there's plenty of stories here to try.

These stories are also tied together by my unifying concept: each one is an excerpt from the strangest day in its characters' lives. Every single story in here is that strange day. We all have strange days where everything seems wrong and nothing seems to fit. They don't always have werewolves in them, but, close enough.

You might have noticed the front cover of this book. Hopefully, you did. This is one instance where I welcome you judging this book by its cover. That painting you can peek through the title there is entitled *Timoclea Kills Captain of Alexander the Great, Her Rapist, by Stuffing Him in Well*. It was painted by Elisabetta Sirani in 1659. I will let the title of the painting speak for the presence of this art on the cover of this book. By the end of the book, I think you will understand why.

This book also explores something I've noticed recently: it's okay to be interested in the weird, the gross, the strange, the horrible. It's okay to look up everything you can about Ted Bundy. It's okay to love every alien science-fiction movie you come across. It's okay to try to solve the mystery of the Zodiac Killer. It's okay to watch every unsolved mystery show on television. It's *okay!* We can like it all in public now! Enjoy this book with your friends. Share it like you share your theories on the murder of JonBenét Ramsey and Jack the Ripper. The world is yours for the taking.

My last message is this: Survive your strange days. Keep moving forwards. Laugh and live and make yourself happy. In the end, you are the only person who you need to please. The only person you need to be better than is the person you were the day before. Process your world. Process yourself. Learn and grow and become a better version of you. Know that I love you. Keep going.

ACKNOWLEDGMENTS

There are always so many people to thank when it comes to projects like these. There is Joanna, who edited my stories and gave stellar encouraging comments, like "love these ladies 2: electric boogaloo." There is Renan, who told me, while I laid face-down murmuring "I'm no good at this," that I am good at this and should keep working. There are my coworkers, who laughed at every ridiculous search I made on our work computer while I was doing research. Examples include "Was Louis XIV handsome?", "do baseball pants have a special name?", and "synonym big." There are my friends, who encouraged and supported me with cornbread, crime shows, and self-care nights. There is my ohana. They're the ones who taught me to write and the ones who tell me to keep writing, even when my more lucrative cousins show up at Thanksgiving having achieved much more than I. One last shout-out to the mess of a world we live in. A lot of this book is dedicated to processing what has been going on in the world around us. So much of it is bad. This book is about destroying the bad, and replacing it with newfound good.

CONTENTS

"One fine day,
in the middle of the night,
Two dead boys
got up to fight;
Back to back
they faced each other,
Drew their swords,
and shot each other."

[Anonymous]

FIDDLE ME TWICE

When the Devil originally goes down to Georgia and challenges Johnny to a fiddling contest, he never expects to lose. Johnny, however, never expects to come into contact with a golden fiddle, much less one gifted to him by the Devil. He's been around the block a few times; he knows not to mess with golden artifacts given to him by Catholic symbols of sin. It's practically step one in being confirmed. So, Johnny leaves it on the ground. He plays "Fire on the Mountain" — on his own fiddle — all the way back home, and dies there decades later, soul very much intact.

Meanwhile, the golden fiddle continues to gather dirt and dust. It ends up underneath the soil, then underneath a misplaced tree; eventually, it's under a fast food joint, as magical golden fiddles in Georgia are wont to do. The magical golden fiddle has no idea what its powers or abilities are. It's a fiddle. It remains under the dirt and roots and chicken sandwiches and unnecessary religious ties until that very fast food joint catches on fire due to a decidedly unmagical and metal-silver fryer burning up the place. When the place is bulldozed and the pavement underneath is torn up, the shredded foundations reveal the very tip of the golden fiddle.

"Now, hold up, there!" Reg calls, jumping from his lawn chair. As the overseer of the site, he has his very own lawn chair, gifted to him by his husband and with a golden *Reginald* painted on the top in ornate puff paint. He hops down into the ravine left behind by the ashes of the fast food place and his own company's diggers and burrows with his nails to unearth the mystery under the dirt. He has a bit of a deja-vu trip to the one and only time he had seen that godforsaken dinosaur movie with that guy with the voice — you know the one? that one — as he lifts the golden fiddle out of the dirt.

"Whatcha got there, Reg?" Dan calls down. Reg holds the golden fiddle high above his head, feeling warmed just by its very presence. It seems to glow. Reg looks it over with the patience and attention he feels it deserves.

"Banjo, I think!" Reg finally tells him. Dan offers him a hand to help him back up to ground level. His team of workers gather around him to see the banjo-cum-fiddle as he brushes the magical years of normal dirt off it.

"Naw," Howie says, near the back of the group. "That ain't no banjo, Mr. Reg. That there's a fiddle."

"Is that solid gold, Mr. Reg?" Barbara Ann asks. Reg skims his fingertip over one of the strings, still in perfect condition.

"I dunno," he tells her. He flips the fiddle over in his hands. "Back says 'Johnny.'" He looks up at the crowd. "Anyone know a Johnny?"

"I'm Johnny," three voices call back. They all step forward, but none of them recognize the banjo (possibly a fiddle) as belonging to them. Candy hops up out of the fast food canyon and hands over a golden stick.

"Found the bow, Mr. Reg," Candy says, handing it over. Reg holds it high, then sets it to the fiddle. Clouds gather overhead abruptly, casting them all in darkness, and Reg frowns at the sky. The moment the bow falls away from the fiddle, the sky clears again, sun blasting down. Testing his theory, he holds the bow up again, and, sure as shit, back come the clouds. He drops the bow; the sun returns.

"Well, fellas," Reg says, examining the golden fiddle. "We can control the weather. What should we do with it?"

"I think we ought to take the day off," Barbara Ann says. "If we make it rain, sir, pardon my sayin' so, but I don't rightly think we'd have to stay, and I'd sure like to get home and watch some television."

Reg's team is made up of a good kind of people, the sort of people Reg likes getting drinks with, allowing time off for, and, now and then, giving magic rain to. With a shrug, Reg sets the bow to the fiddle once more, the clouds gathering yet again and sending the construction site into pitch-blackness. He plays one screeching note on the fiddle and the rain starts pouring down, sure enough, but it doesn't hit any of them. Indeed, a circle of dry air forms around them, keeping them untouched by the torrent. Reg pulls back and frowns at the rain.

"Well, I'll be damned," he says, and lightning strikes the ground beside him. When he jumps back to get out of the way, he stumbles into a body far larger than his own. He steps back. "Pardon me, sir."

"No trouble," says the much larger man. Upon Reg's closer inspection, he turns out not to be so much of a man at all, but actually perhaps a demon or devil of some sort. Reg glances down at his feet and finds the cloven hooves he's come to expect. His skin is of a nice red tint, like a good cherry might have, and his horns are fairly obvious on top of his head.

"You some sort of devil?" Reg asks. The cherry man-beast glowers at him.

"I am *the* Devil," he says, and Reg takes off his construction helmet.

"My apologies," Reg says, because he knows that you don't piss off the Devil. It's practically step two in being confirmed. "May I ask what you're doing here, Mr. Devil?"

The Devil points at the fiddle. "You've found my fiddle and played it. In doing so, Reginald Alma Hanberry, you have challenged me to a fiddling contest."

"I hate to disagree with you, Mr. Devil, but I've done no such thing," Reg says. The Devil hesitates, then points again at the fiddle.

"You did play a note on this fiddle, yes?"

"I sure did," Reg says.

"And was it an F?"

"I don't know, sir. I'm awful sorry," Reg says.

"Then you've challenged me."

Reg shakes his head. "I'm sorry, but I haven't challenged you. This may be your fiddle, and I may have played a note on it, and that note may have been an F, but one thing I surely didn't do was challenge the Devil to a fiddling contest."

"You don't have to do it with the intention of challenging me," the Devil informs him. "It's just the rule of the fiddle."

"That hardly seems fair," Barbara Ann calls. Candy nods.

"Babs' got a point, Mr. Devil," Howie says. "That there fiddle was under the restaurant. How'd we even know the damn thing's yours? Pardon my Godly French."

"It says 'Johnny' on the back," Dan says. "Is your name Johnny, Mr. Devil?"

"No," the Devil says. The crowd murmurs. "Now, hold on, hear me out. Many years ago, on this very swath of land, I challenged a young fiddler named Johnny to a fiddling contest. The bet was his soul."

"Oh, that's a risky bet," Howie says. "I wouldn't bet my soul on a fiddle."

"So, this was Johnny's fiddle?" Reg asks.

"I'd bet my soul on *that* fiddle," Candy says.

"The bet was his soul," the Devil repeats firmly, "and I lost the bet. He was a better fiddler than I, and so he won my golden fiddle. However, it seems that he did not take his prize with him."

"Now, that's a damn shame," Reg says, forgetting his to excuse his own Godly French. "Who'd leave this behind? At least try to hock it."

"I'd've hocked it by now if I were you, Reg," Howie says. Reg motions towards the Devil with the bow of the fiddle.

"I can't rightly do that with the Devil right there claimin' it's his, now, can I, Howie?" Reg asks, and Howie shrugs. Johnny

21

puts a hand on Howie's shoulder. A different Johnny steps forward.

"So, Reg owes you his soul?" Johnny asks. The third Johnny leans around to look at the Devil's face. Reg feels a little bad for arguing with him; he's pretty sure not arguing with the Devil might be step three in being confirmed. On the other hand, though, he does want to keep his soul.

"Reginald owes me his soul if he loses our bet," the Devil says.

"But we ain't made no bet," Reg reminds him. The Devil's fists clench.

"You made the challenge by playing the fiddle."

"But I ain't-"

"*Reginald*," the Devil thunders. "Do you dare question the word of the Devil?"

"I suppose not," Reg says. The Devil raises his hand to the air, and a silver fiddle appears in his skillet-sized palm. He lifts the fingers of his other hand and a bow materializes between them. "Who goes first, then?"

"You do," the Devil says, likely having learned his lesson from letting Johnny go second all those years ago. Reg shrugs and steps back, lifting the bow to the fiddle.

"Here goes nothing, boys," says Reg, and he scrapes on one string. The Devil clamps his hands over his ears.

"Jesus Christ, Reginald, what the Hell was that?" the Devil demands. Barbara Ann titters behind her hand.

"Y'all don't like my fiddle playin'?" Reg asks, seeming a little crestfallen. Dan pats him on the back.

"Now, Reg, it wasn't so bad," Dan tells him. Howie nods. "I think you just need some practice, is all."

"Can he have some time to practice?" Candy asks. The whole construction team looks up at the Devil, waiting for an answer.

"I honestly don't think all the time in the world would help," the Devil tells them.

"And how much time is that?" asks Johnny, seizing on an opportunity. The Devil ignores him.

"Since you stopped playing, I get to play now," the Devil says, seeming awfully sure of himself. Reg steps out of the way of his tremendous and pointed elbow to allow him the space to play. He moves his bow to the fiddle and immediately snaps the strings. The whole team falls silent.

"Wow," Howie whispers.

"You have got to be *fucking* kidding me," the Devil spits. He throws his fiddle and bow to the ground, where they turn to gold. "Fine. *Fine.* You win, Reginald."

"Really?" Reg asks. Dan picks up the Devil's second golden fiddle and second golden bow. The strings apparently repaired themselves mid-transformation. "Even though it didn't sound so good?"

"Technically, you won, because I didn't even get to make a bad note," the Devil says, "but I still did touch my bow to the fiddle."

"Seems like a *really* specific rule for a soul-bet fiddle-contest," Candy says. The Devil turns to her.

"Do you want me to take Reginald's soul?" he asks. She shakes her head.

"No, sir."

"How about yours, then?"

"No, sir."

"Then zip it," he says. He turns back to Reg and bows his head. "Congratulations, Reginald. You have defeated me in this, our great fiddle contest. You get to keep your soul and my *second* golden fiddle." He raises his hands and the rain stops; the clouds clear, letting the sun shine through again. The Devil seems much shorter in the light.

"Well, thanks, you old son of a bitch," Reg says. He lets Dan stack the second golden fiddle on top of the first. "Can I sell 'em?"

"I don't care," the Devil says, and vanishes with a crack and a cloud of sulfur. Barbara Ann waves her hands to disperse the smoke.

"Well, congrats, Reg," Dan says. Howie punches Reg on the arm.

"What're you gonna do with the fiddles?" Johnny asks. Reg looks the fiddles and the bows over. He thinks absently that beating the Devil in a fiddle contest was never taught to him before his confirmation.

"Well," says Reg, "I reckon I'll hock one, but I'll keep the other."

"Why'd you wanna keep one?" Candy asks. Reg shrugs.

"If I ever accidentally play one again," Reg says, "I guess I better know how to really play. It should work alright if I use a regular bow, that's how I figure it. I'd rather not go to Hell if I can help it, thanks."

And so the golden fiddle and its twin fall into the possession of Reginald Alma Hanberry, construction manager and first of his name, until the twin fiddle falls into the hands of the pawn shop down the road and the possession of Charles John Daniels, who melts it and its bow down to make a bunch of gold jewelry to sell in his shop. Reg spends the rest of his days attempting to play the fiddle, but he only ever succeeds in learning the tuba after his retirement down the street from a brand-new fast food joint. He sheds his mortal coil with his soul intact, and so it is the rumor around that Georgia town for years to come that the Devil came to fear Reg's violin playing. In reality, it is only that the Devil had run out of golden fiddles, and always thinks it best to ignore Reg's final escapades.

SEVEN DEADLY SONS

Jason is the oldest son of the King of Hell, but he had been born before his father fell, so he is both hot and has a moral compass. He also has seven younger brothers, whom he loves deeply, but who struggle to get along with him. His younger brothers had been planned; with names like Lust, or Envy, or Gluttony, how can you not be? Jason, however, had been an unplanned explosion of grace that had resulted in a son just months before the Fall, and so he is imbued with the entirety of the seven virtues. Jason, the Crown Prince of Hell, is drenched in the qualities Heaven values most: prudence, justice, temperance, courage, faith, hope, and charity. His brothers do not approve of him. His father, largely, does not approve of him. Jason loves them all anyways, as is his lot in life.

Jason also has no fucking idea what he's doing. His father is on death's door, ready to pass on to whichever realm comes next, which means Jason is next in line to be King of Hell, which *means* he has to learn how to be King of Hell.

"Despite our best efforts," Lucifer tells his saintly son, before the entirety of the court, "you are set to be crowned King tomorrow."

"Thank you, Father," Jason says. Envy rolls his eyes at his older brother, there on his knees on the stone. He is the only one of the brothers to show up to the meeting. He hopes his other brothers are busy with the plan he has in motion, since *obviously* Jason can't survive until his own coronation and *obviously* Envy is a more reasonable choice for their father's successor.

"Have you practiced your oath?" Lucifer asks over the low strains of jazz filling the room. Jason nods. "And you have crafted your sceptre and pitchfork?"

"I have," Jason tells him. "I'm ready to do anything you ask of me."

Lucifer groans audibly. The council laughs, titters that echo through the candlelit chamber. Jason continues kneeling obediently, head bowed.

"Kid," Lucifer says. "You're killing me here." He leans forwards. "Look, I get it. I was born in Heaven, too. It sucks, being that good, doesn't it?"

Jason doesn't say anything, but he does lift his head, glancing at his father.

"No," he says, and Lucifer sighs, leaning back.

"You've always been a lost cause," Lucifer says. Jason drops his head again; Envy wonders if this is what shame looks like. "Have you chosen a consort?" Lucifer asks, and Jason shakes his head. "How about an heir?"

"My eldest brother," Jason answers, and Envy scoffs. It's the *law,* and yet he responds like he has made some godly decision all on his own.

"Envy, you accept this role?" Lucifer asks. Envy nods.

"Yup," he says. "We'll see how long it lasts."

Another laugh. Jason doesn't even look up at his brother. Envy wishs he would, then looks away to his father again.

"Then I will see you in the morning, Jason," Lucifer says. He smacks his own sceptre against the stone floor, filling the room with a horrible, echoing clatter. "You're dismissed."

"Thank you, Father," Jason says, rising to his feet. He offers him a bow, then leaves the room, his eyes lingering on Envy only for a moment. Envy stares back, unblinking. Jason leaves.

"I hope you're hard at work, my son," Lucifer says to Envy, an aside not meant to be heard by the rest of the council, though they likely know what he's talking about. Envy stands from his throne.

"Trust me," Envy says, before leaving. He passes by the sin branding room, full of new souls getting their disgraces burnt onto their chests, then by the soul-stripping room, containing the freshly dead getting cored of their souls, of their very beings, in much the way apples get their middles sucked out for consumption. Next, they get sent off to their own personal hells, hand-crafted by an office full of the worst demons his father can find, but Envy takes a left instead, down the halls of his brothers. He finds Lust easily enough, because if he knows one sound in the world, he knows the sound of his brother howling through the castle.

"Get out," Envy orders the other bodies he finds, as soon as he discovers them. Knowing better, everyone scatters, leaving Lust alone on the floor.

"What the fuck do you want?" Lust asks, heaving himself to his feet. Envy knocks him back down.

"You have a job to do," Envy snarls. "Why aren't you fucking doing it?"

"It's already done, Jesus Christ, get off my back," Lust groans, kicking out at his brother's ankles. Envy sidesteps him easily.

"You couldn't've helped someone else? Just had to come back here?" Envy asks. Lust waves him off, standing up again and pulling his robes on.

"Gluttony is done, Sloth is done, Wrath and Pride are still setting up their parts of it," Lust tells him.

"How about Greed?" Envy asks. Lust shrugs. "What, you can't keep tabs on him?"

"Isn't that your fucking job?" Lust asks. "Leave me alone, holy shit, you're always up my *ass*."

"You'd know, you put everything up your fucking ass," Envy spits, already leaving the room. "Where's Greed?"

"I told you I don't *fucking know,*" Lust screams at him. Envy hears something hit the wall near the door and shatter as he leaves. He strides down the hall and nearly slams right into Jason, who seems too lost in his own head to be focused on where he is.

"Oh," Jason says. "Sorry, I didn't—"

"Move," Envy snarls, and Jason doesn't, not at first. "Look—"

"I know tomorrow is a big day," Jason says, instead. "I know you didn't want it to happen like this. I wanted to talk to you about it, actually."

"What's there to talk about?" Envy asks. "You're going to be King, and that's—"

"That's the thing," Jason says. "I don't— I really don't think I'm cut out for it. I want to abdicate."

Envy stops trying to shove past his brother to stare at him instead. "What?"

"I want to abdicate," Jason repeats. "I think you'd be better at it. I don't think I'm meant for a job like that. You can assign me wherever you'd like, but I think you should do it instead. I know Father prefers you, and, honestly, so do I, for this."

"What?" Envy says again. Jason claps his hand on his brother's shoulder.

"I'll do it at the coronation tomorrow," Jason says. "I know you've wanted it. I'm so proud of who you've become. I have faith in you."

Jason passes him by and continues down the hall to his chambers. Envy feels extremely complicated. He hurries down the hall to Greed's room, ignoring the strangest feeling of needing to please his eldest brother.

"Get up," Envy orders, as soon as the door bangs open. Greed looks up from his painting on the floor. "We have to stop our plan."

"What?" Greed demands, already on his feet. "Why? We're going to execute it perfectly. It's already in place."

"He wants to abdicate," Envy tells him. "I'll get the throne anyways."

"So?" Greed says. "He pisses me off. We should've done this a long time ago."

Envy stares at him. Greed stares back.

"What?" he asks again. "If you're having second thoughts—"

"Fuck you," Envy snaps, then leaves. He slams the door shut behind him and leans against it, catching his breath. His chest stirs. He gathers himself, then starts for Jason's chambers, wondering how, exactly, he would get him to leave without anything happening to him.

It is, as it turns out, too late.

He hears Jason cry out, and he breaks into a sprint, slamming open the door. He finds Pride already there, standing before Jason, who is shackled to the floor, one dagger in his shoulder-blade, unmoving.

"Don't do this," Jason is saying, as the door bounces heavily off the wall. He looks to Envy. "Please. Don't. You don't know—"

"Shut up," Sloth says lazily from the corner, kicking his feet up over the arm of the chair. "You had to know this was coming."

"He's planning to—"

"No," Wrath says, stepping forward. Lust slips past Envy to get into the room. Jason just looks up at him, distraught, all blood-mouth and big eyes. "It's been time for this. He knew it was coming."

"Please," Jason says. Wrath lifts his longsword.

"No," Envy says, then, loudly, *"No,"* but is too late, or Wrath doesn't care to listen as he drives the blade down through their brother's back. Jason keeps his eye contact with Envy, choking, dying on the floor, seven minutes left to go until total death. Envy stares at him, then wants, intensely, to die the same way.

"What's done is done," Greed says from the doorway, as Wrath pushes the sword in a little more. Envy glares at him.

"What the fuck is wrong with you?" Envy demands, still staring at Jason's face. "I *told* you—"

"It doesn't matter what he said," Wrath tells him. "It doesn't matter what he wanted to do. It doesn't even matter what he actually does. He's never belonged here. *Never.*"

"Like shit he didn't," Envy says. "He's the best of us."

"*Hello?*" Wrath exclaims. "Look around you, buddy. We're in *Hell*. The 'best of us' doesn't deserve to be the *King of Hell.*" Wrath twists the sword around a little bit. Jason coughs, and Envy glances back down at him. Jason's eyes are shutting, slowly, like he's drowsy, and his head lists to the side a little.

"Oh, don't look at him like that," Greed says. "It's no big loss. He'll go right back up to Heaven and live happily ever after. He never should've been down here, anyways."

"It *doesn't matter,*" Envy spits. "It doesn't. It just doesn't. He *was* here, so it just—"

"Grow up, you fucking moron," Sloth chimes in. "People die. It's our job."

Envy glares at him, then back to Jason, who stares at him with the last of the energy he has left. Wrath checks his watch.

"That should do it," Wrath says. Envy steps forward and shoves him back.

"Don't you dare," Envy says. Wrath catches his balance and comes right back at him.

"Don't I dare *what?*" Wrath asks. "He's already dead. I'm just finishing the job."

"Like hell you are," Envy replies. Wrath raises an eyebrow at him and wraps his hand around the handle of the longsword. Envy smacks his wrist, and Wrath pulls back to punch him across the jaw. Envy stumbles backwards, skittering to one knee, hand over his face. By the time he catches himself and looks up, Wrath has two hands around the base of the longsword.

"Don't—" Envy says, his throat drying up all at once. Wrath ignores him completely, even as Envy stumbles to his feet and attempts to come after him; Greed grabs his hands and yanks him backwards again. Envy, forced to his knees, is face-to-face with Jason. Jason just smiles and shakes his head.

"It's going to be okay," he says, blood spilling out of his mouth the second he opens it, flowing onto the floor like it came from an overturned glass. It drips from his chin in slow drops after that, and Wrath braces himself, yanking the longsword out of Jason's chest. Jason gasps, tipping back onto his haunches. Envy struggles, trying to get free, to take it himself if he has to, but he can't. Instead, Wrath cleanly, without a care in the goddamned world, lops their brother's head off. It smacks heavily into the floor and rolls to face Envy.

There is a beat of total silence, as Envy stares down into Jason's unblinking eyes, at the blood seeping out of the open wound that had been his neck and throat.

The warning bells strung through the halls start clanging all at once, and Envy's attention snaps around to Wrath. There's only one reason those bells would ring: a creature from Heaven has arrived. The only Heavenly creature Envy can think of is his brother. He yanks himself out of Greed's grasp.

"He went to Hell," Envy says. "Holy shit. He came back. How the fuck—"

"We should've disabled the fucking heavenly alarms," Wrath says. "We didn't think there was a chance he'd end up back down here, I didn't think—"

"*How the fuck did he end up in Hell?*" Envy demands. Wrath shrugs, carefree in a way Envy has always craved feeling.

"Honestly, it doesn't even matter," Wrath says. "He's dead. He's gone, it's over. Nobody gives a shit."

"Fuck you," Envy snaps. He flees the room to the soul-stripping room, only to see his brother's bloody back as it passes through into the sin branding room. He shoulders the door open and finds his brother, head in his hands, eyes blinking up at him.

"It's okay," Jason says, as his brand is prepared. His mouth is held down near his waist; Envy stares at the open wound of his neck, at what so recently was a whole form. "It is. I knew it was coming. I knew."

"But—"

"I forgive you," Jason says. He looks from Envy to the judge before him, who is perusing the tome of Jason's life. The judge looks back at him, and Jason returns the scrutiny, the two of them staring into each other's insides. Jason's eyes flicker to Envy, and the judge sighs, as if this seals some deal for him. He flicks the book shut, lifts one of the brands along his desk up, and sticks the thing into the tiny fire beside him. Jason keeps eye contact with Envy as the brand is pressed into his skin.

IDOLATRY, it reads, in crisped skin, singed to the bone. "I've always loved you. All of you, and Father, but you the most."

Envy's heart seizes. He had no idea where his heart was even placed in his chest before this moment, when Jason looks him in the face, *IDOLATRY* blazing on his chest, and forces him to know that this was all his fault.

"Jason—"

"It's okay," Jason says again. Envy feels his chest pulse. "It's fine. It was always going to be this way. I know who you are."

Jason is escorted from the room, to be taken to whatever personal hell is now his, and Envy stands there, watching, waiting for his return. It never comes.

MARAUDERS

Captain Phineas Woodbury has seen a lot in his days.
He's been a pirate for a long, long time. Things don't surprise
him anymore.

"How in the hell did you do this?" Phineas asks.
Quartermaster Abraham Hawkins grins, kicking his feet up on
the table in the captain's quarters.

"I've been holding onto it for when we had some time
alone," Abe says. Phineas uses a knife to open the bottle of perry.

"I haven't had a good pear cider in Lord knows how
long," Phineas tells him. Abe keeps grinning at him, rocking his
chair back and forth on the back two legs.

"I know," he says. He lets his chair slam to the ground,
drops his legs to the floor, and stands, coming behind Phineas.
Phineas leans his head back against Abe's chest, lets him scratch

at his scalp, massage his shoulders. "You've been stressed out. I know you love perry. You needed it."

"I love you, too," Phineas says. Abe kisses the crown of his head and keeps rubbing at his shoulders. "Want some?"

"Hell yes," Abe tells him. He takes the bottle from Phineas' hands and lifts it up above his head, taking a long sip from it. Someone slams into the door of the captain's quarters, and Abe stops drinking, raising a questioning eyebrow at the door.

"Get the door, please," Phineas says, and Abe goes, leaving the perry behind. Phineas takes another sip while Abe opens the door.

"Captain, there's a ship out there," one of the new shiphands says. They only just picked him up at the last port; Phineas thinks his name might be Hannibal. "In the fog. Her name says she's the *Diamond.*"

"I've never heard of her," Phineas tells him. "Is she a threat?"

"She's heading right for us, Captain," Hannibal says. "She's not slowing down or turning. I'm concerned about her."

"Then I'll come and investigate." Phineas stands from his desk and follows Hannibal out of the captain's quarters and up the stairs, above deck. He can feel Abe following right behind him. All of the men are on deck, staring in the same direction. One of them gives Phineas his telescope.

"That way, Captain," Hannibal tells him, pointing, and Phineas holds the telescope up and searches through the fog. He doesn't need to search for long; he finds the *Diamond* easily. She's slicing through the fog, heading directly for them. He's seen a lot in his days. He's never seen a ship that looked ready to slice them both in two.

"Good Lord, turn away," Phineas tells his crew. A couple of men run for the wheel. "What do they think they're *doing?*"

"This is suicide," Abe comments at his left. Phineas hands him the telescope. "See, that's just stupid. I—" Abe falls silent, and, when Phineas glances at him, he's frowning. "There's nobody on board."

"What?" Phineas asks. Abe gives the telescope back to him.

"There's nobody on board," Abe repeats, and Phineas looks through the telescope at the deck of the *Diamond*. Abe's not telling the truth; there is somebody on board.

"There's a woman," Phineas says. The men all lean, trying to get a better look. "Balance yourselves out, men, my God, you're going to tip us over."

The men spread themselves over the deck of the ship, all trying to see the woman on the *Diamond*. She stands on the forecastle, staring straight ahead, with a young boy at her side. There are no crewmembers in sight. It is an entirely unsettling thing to see.

"God, there's a woman and a child," Phineas tells the crew. They all murmur to each other, passing the word back through the crowd of men. "That's it. Those are the only people on board."

"Maybe the crew is below deck," Hannibal suggests.

"And just left a woman on top to commit suicide by slamming into another ship?" Abe asks. "Think with your head, Hannibal. Something's wrong with this."

"Damn straight, something's wrong," Phineas agrees. He slams the telescope shut and hands it over to Hannibal. He turns to his crew. "Pull the ship about and prepare to board the *Diamond*. We'll figure out what's going on and help if necessary. If unnecessary, we rob her blind and let her go kill someone else's ship. Agreed?"

"Aye!" the men shout back, and scatter to do as he says. Abe stays at Phineas' side, leaning back against the rail. Phineas turns back to the sea to watch the *Diamond*.

"This is weird," Abe comments. Phineas glances at him. "Not your fault. I'm just saying." He looks over his shoulder. "You sure you wanna get tangled with that thing?"

"I'm *so* curious," Phineas tells him. Abe laughs and claps him on the shoulder.

"That doesn't surprise me," Abe says. "That's a horrendously *you* reason to just board a bizarre ship in the fog at night."

Phineas nods, still watching the ship as it heads for them. She doesn't change course, doesn't divert, doesn't turn. She's moving ahead, straight ahead, in a perfect line. Phineas has no idea how she's doing that with one woman and one child for a crew. There's absolutely no way.

Eventually, Phineas' ship — the *Lady James* — turns away, and they pull alongside the *Diamond*. The two ships drift ever closer, until, soon, they are side-by-side. Phineas has his men fetch a gangplank and place it between the two ships so he and half of his crew may board the *Diamond*. Abe follows at Phineas' right hand, looking unsettled. He's taking everything in so Phineas doesn't have to; Phineas is the front, the people-person, the voice, while Abe is the strategizer, the planner, the thinker.

Even Phineas notices, though, that the ship is almost entirely deserted. There's nobody left on board save the woman and child they saw from a distance, and they're slowly approaching, the woman ahead with the boy's hand in hers, leading him down to the upper deck, where Phineas and his men stand and await them.

"Hello!" Phineas calls to them. Neither of them answers. Phineas glances to Abe, who half-shrugs. The both of them look back to the woman at the same time. "Hello? Are you alright?"

"Miss?" Abe asks. The woman just keeps her steady pace.

"Oh, Lord, she's dead," one of the crewmen says.

"She's a goddamned ghost," another men says.

"Hush," Abe whispers behind Phineas' back. "Shut up, all of you. She's not dead." Abe turns back to Phineas. "Is she dead?"

"She can't be, she's walking," Phineas says. Abe snorts.

"Sea spirits are not common, but they must exist," Abe tells him. "Otherwise, there wouldn't be stories about them."

"That's terribly faulty logic," Phineas says. "She's fine. See? She's walking over."

"Without talking or breaking pace," Abe points out. It's true; she's gotten closer, still walking steadily, unstopping. The boy follows. She's wearing a grand gown, something Phineas doesn't think has been in style for decades, now. She has white-blonde hair, tangled from the sea winds, and some sort of birthmark on her face, near her mouth. The boy, too, is similarly white-blonde, similarly well-dressed, with a similar birthmark near his mouth. Their eyes are sunken and bruised; their skin looks sallow.

"They look ill," Phineas says. "Did Martha come with us? We may need her help treating them."

"Can't fix dead," someone comments behind Phineas. Abe turns and whacks them on the arm.

"*Shut up,*" Abe orders them, quietly, as the woman stops before Phineas.

"Hello," Phineas says again. He looks down at the boy. "And hello to you, too. What's your name?"

"Jonah," the boy says. His voice echoes for no reason at all, since they're in the open sea air.

"Jonah," Phineas repeats. "It's a pleasure. Is this your mother?"

"Yes," Jonah says. Phineas looks closer at his face. The birthmark isn't a birthmark. There's blood around the boy's mouth. Phineas glances up at the woman's face; she's got blood there, too. Phineas hopes to *death* it's their own blood.

"And what's your name?" Phineas asks of the woman.

"Louise," the boy answers for her.

"Miss Louise," Phineas says. He reaches for her hand. She doesn't move to offer it, nor to withdraw it, and so Phineas just lifts it up in his and kisses the back of it. He usually does it as a show of good faith, charisma, comradery, what have you. He immediately wishes he had not done it this time, because her hand is bony and freezing cold. He lets go as soon as he politely can. "We noticed you don't have a crew on board. Are you in need of help?"

"No," Louise says. She looks down at Jonah. "Do not speak to them."

"Sorry," Jonah tells her. He stares straight ahead at the crew, hand still held tightly in his mother's. Louise looks back up at Phineas.

"Get off my ship," Louise says. Phineas feels a chill go down his spine.

"You look horribly ill," Phineas says. "We have a physician on board. We want to help, if someone's gone wrong. Has something gone wrong?"

"Get off my ship," Louise repeats. Phineas glances back to Abe, whose face has gone a bit pale.

"We're just worried about you," Phineas says, turning back to Louise. "The way you were steering this ship, it's suicide—"

"Get off my ship," Louise shrieks. The deck seems to flicker, like a candle flame. Phineas blinks and raises his hands up, palms-out.

"I don't want to hurt you," Phineas tells her. "I don't. You're safe. I'm not going to hurt you."

"Get off my ship, get *off my ship*—" Louise repeats. She lifts the hand not wrapped up in her son's and curls her fingers into a fist, and the deck flickers again. There are dozens of transparent bodies lying all over the upper deck, throats torn open, limbs with chunks taken out of them. Phineas can't stop staring at them.

"You see?" Jonah asks.

"Get off my ship," Louise says again.

"Did you kill these men?" Abe asks. Phineas takes a step, sliding himself to the side so he's halfway in front of Abe, ready to defend him.

"Yes," Jonah tells them.

"Shh," Louise murmurs, softly, and the boy falls silent again. She looks back up at the men. "Yes."

"Why?" Abe asks.

"Get off my ship," Louise repeats. Phineas feels Abe back up a step, so he glances backwards; the men are already edging back towards the gangplank.

"It's not worth it," one of the men calls to Phineas from the back. "Captain, let's go."

"I want to help," Phineas says. He turns back to Louise. "I want to help. Will you let me help you?"

"You can't," Louise tells him.

"Sure, I can," Phineas says. "I absolutely can. We have food and a physician and a full crew. We can bring you to land. Would you like that?"

"No," Louise says. Phineas takes a step forward, and Louise spits at him. "Get off my ship."

"We'll eat you, too," Jonah tells them.

"Oh, God, they ate them," Abe whispers. "Phineas, let's go—"

"Get off my ship," Louise repeats. Phineas stumbles back a step, hand going towards his pistol, and Louise flies forward, dragging Jonah with her as she grabs Phineas' arm and yanks at it, taking a bite of his wrist. Phineas shouts and kicks at her, shoving her backwards, as crewmembers dart forward to tear them apart.

"Get off!" Louise shrieks at them. Abe drags Phineas backwards, the two of them going stumbling off the ship. She slips through the hands of the crewmen who try to hold her, tugging her son backwards. "Go. Get out."

"We want to help," Phineas calls to her, even as Abe keeps hauling him back towards the *Lady James*.

"You can't," Louise says. Her voice is soft and sad and angry. Her fist clenches again, and both her face and Jonah's flicker into skulls. Phineas can see straight through to their bones, then out the other side of them. "You can't help us. Do you see?"

"Christ," Phineas says, and Abe tugs him across the gangplank. They pull the gangplank up and start sailing again, unable to move fast enough to satisfy the primal urge to get away. Phineas looks out at the *Diamond* as they pull away, cutting back through the night's dark waves. He can't stop staring, and Louise and Jonah stare back, bloodied, sunken eyes unblinking.

"Almighty God," Phineas breathes. Abe's hand wraps around his elbow and lifts his arm, examining the spot where the chunk of flesh was ripped from him. The *Diamond* vanishes into the fog, like it was never there. Phineas looks down at his arm; the edges of the wound are blackened. She bit right down to the bone; he can see white through the blood.

"We have to take you to Martha," Abe tells him. Phineas lets himself be dragged below deck to his quarters. Abe rushes off to retrieve Martha, but all Phineas can see behind his closed eyes are the faces of Louise and Jonah, still staring at him, from the other side.

But Satisfaction Brought It Back

Kristian stops in the town square to listen to the cryer, who is screaming so loudly Kris thinks it's a bird when he's coming down the mountain.

"If you consider yourself brave," shrieks the cryer, "then report to Georgie's Tavern at once!"

Kris considers this. He thinks of his empty cabin in the woods, outside of town, and he thinks of the warmth of the tavern, and maybe of a free drink if they think he is "brave enough." He drops the tree he's dragging to the carpenter's place and shakes out his arms.

"What's this for, anyways?" asks Adrian, one of the tailor's apprentices, of the cryer. Kris looks Adrian up, and down; a moron like him isn't stiff competition.

"Carver'll tell you if you go to Georgie's," the cryer tells him, before moving down the street to repeat his message. Adrian glances to Kris, shrugs, and heads for Georgie's. Kris watches him disappear out of the snow into the warm wood building before he hefts his tree back onto his shoulder and heads once more towards the carpenter's. He delivers his tree and receives only half his from the carpenter who never keeps his promises. Now, with his night wide open, he heads to Georgie's.

Adrian is not the only one in town who considers himself brave, it seems. Carver, the squire of the duke who legally owns their village lands, is seated in a chair on top of a table, surrounded by a handful of the town's largest or most confident citizens.

Kris stands in the doorway a moment, relishing in the way people turn to look at him, how they have to crane their necks to see his face. He has been lonely for a long time; he enjoys how little he cares about what they think, at this point in his life. He tips his head to Bryony behind the bar, who frowns at him like he's a stray dog and looks away. The wind blows the door shut behind him.

"I was wondering if you'd show," Adrian's nasal voice calls to him. Kris grunts at him and sits down in a recently-vacated chair, ignoring how it creaks underneath him. "Carver was just about to explain what we're all doing here, ain't he?"

"Yes," Carver, who Kris privately thinks of as The Duke's Pissant, says, with the air of someone who thinks he's important despite regularly being told otherwise. "I have a quest."

"A quest?" snorts Ruthie, the blacksmith. "What kind of fucking fairy-tale story is this?"

"Let him talk," Adrian snaps. Ruthie, that phenomenal bitch, yanks him into a headlock. The Duke's Pissant pretends not to notice the antics of less civilized beings as he looks down on them all from his perch.

"The Duke would like the castle cleared," The Duke's Pissant says, and the tavern falls silent in waves as the crowd processes what he said.

"The castle?" Adrian asks. "The *castle* castle? Up on the ledge?"

"You know another one, dipshit?" Ruthie asks. Bryony comes out from behind the bar and wedges herself between them to prevent further scuffling.

"You know that place's got a monster in it, right?" said Wilson. "Like, a beast. Big one. My da saw it once."

Kris glances to his left, then his right. People go quiet and all creased-faced when he looks at them. He turns his attention back up to The Duke's Pissant.

"Thank you... sir," The Duke's Pissant says, barely looking at Kris. Kris doesn't move. "Okay," The Duke's Pissant continues. "Beast or not, The Duke wants it cleared. He anticipated your reluctance. That's why we ask that the bravest among you goes first. The second-place winner goes after him, if he can't succeed, and so on."

"I vote for myself," Adrian exclaims, leaping to his feet. Ruthie glares at him.

"This is not a democracy," The Duke's Pissant says. "Sit down, Archer."

"Adrian," Adrian corrects, but The Duke's Pissant has already moved on.

"You must perform a feat of strength," The Duke's Pissant says. "Not only of body, but also," he taps his temple, "of mind."

"I think you should use Kristian," Bryony, now back behind the bar, tells him, nearly cutting him off but too smart to try it. She glances at Kris, then away, like she doesn't want to look him in the eye while she offers him up as a whipping boy. "He's our biggest."

"That doesn't mean he's your smartest," The Duke's Pissant says, looking Kris over like he's a hunk of meat. Kris weighs his options, looks around the room full of neighbors he hated, then stands up. Once he reaches his full height, he looks down at The Duke's Pissant, meeting him dead in the eye.

"What do we get if we clear the castle?" Kris asks. The Duke's Pissant stares up at him. "Sir?"

The Duke's Pissant clears his throat. "Money."

Kris raises an eyebrow.

"How much money?" Wilson asks. "We make money here just fine."

"More than just fine," The Duke's Pissant says. "A year's wages."

"A *year's wages?*" Bryony behind the bar exclaims, as the room explodes with excited murmuring. Kris continues eyeing The Duke's Pissant, skeptical.

"And all we have to do is clear the castle?" Kris asks. The Duke's Pissant nodded.

"That's all," he says. "Just clear it, come back to us, and tell us when you've done it."

"You don't want proof?" Kris asks.

"We'll have proof enough," The Duke's Pissant tells him. "We'll check once you return." Carter eyes him. "*If* you return."

Kris glances about again, then picks up one of the pewter tankards off the table and takes a long drink from it. People stare. He enjoys having that sort of effect on people, especially people like his fellow villagers.

"I'll do it," he says, at last, in the growing silence. The Duke's Pissant frowns and stands up from his chair, onto the table.

"We have to have the trial first," The Duke's Pissant says, and Kris looms closer, satisfied in how his shadow darkens The Duke's Pissant's entire self.

"I won," Kris says, in as deep a voice as he can manage without practicing first. The Duke's Pissant stares at him, apparently weighing how much Kris cares about his title as The Duke's squire against how far Kris could throw him.

"We'll hold a trial for second place," The Duke's Pissant announces at last, "and for time's sake, we'll send Kristian up tonight. The sooner the better."

"Good idea," Kris says, finishing off what little is left of the tankard and setting it down in front of Adrian. He turns, winks at a scowling Bryony who is, now and forevermore, still behind the bar, and leaves, yanking the door back open. As the cold, snowy breeze rushes into the tavern, he glances back at The Duke's Pissant.

"If I'm not back in three days," he says, "find yourself a new champion."

"Oh, so now the stupid fucking woodsman's our *champion?*" Kris hears Wilson ask, but he slams the door forcefully enough that Wilson probably doesn't ask again. Kris heads for the armory first, stopping in to ask after their strongest weapons. He has only heard about the beast secondhand — from Wilson's da, when Kris himself was still small — but he knows the thing is supposed to be massive, clever, and extraordinarily violent. Next is the tailor for warm clothes and sturdy shoes, then the baker for food supplies. They all seem pleased to hear of his imminent departure.

Armed with two long blades, four short blades, a new set of fur-lined clothes, sturdy boots, a basket full of food strapped to his back, and not a single coin in his pockets, Kris sets on the path up the mountain. He already lives halfway between the castle and the town, so he hardly breaks a sweat during the first half. He tugs his hood and scarf closer around his face and ducks his head against the snow and roaring winds, following his feet up, up through the darkness, up through the trees, against the darkness, and to the ledge that holds the castle.

The castle, Kris thinks, is truly just a large stone house, but it has pointed roofs and heavy carved rocks glued together for walls, so it earns the name *castle* based on the feelings it gives people alone. It doesn't seem so big to Kris, but, then again, nothing seems that big to Kris. He listens closely, or tries to; the howling winds that whip against his head drown out any other sounds he might otherwise hear.

Like any civilized man, he tries the door first.

No answer.

He pushes it open — a heavy wooden thing, with brass knockers and all — and calls out, "Is anyone here?"

Still, no answer.

Kris pushes the door open all the way and then lets it slam shut behind him, of its own accord, leaving him in darkness. He digs in his pockets for one of his last bundles of tinder, and strikes it on his boot, lighting the sticks up in his hand. He finds his way to a torch on the wall, seemingly unused for quite some time, and lights it, illuminating the whole entry hall.

"Hello?" Kris calls out, picking the torch off the wall and holding it high in front of him. The shadows from the fire flicker across the gray stone, but reveal no other person.

"*Leave,*" he hears; a soft whisper, like it is carried on the wind. Kris turns around, but sees no one. He hears it too clearly to believe it just a trick of the breeze, or of his own mind, and glances about the room, wary.

"I can't leave," Kris says. "I have a job."

"*Get out,*" he hears this time. He forges forwards, ignoring the frantic, rhythmic thrum of "*get out, get out, get out*" that follows him to the next door. And then he shoves the wooden door with his shoulder, nearly splintering it in his wake.

"I have to clear the castle," Kris tells this disembodied voice. "I'm assuming you're the monster."

"I am," whispers the voice. *"Leave, now."*

"I don't think so," says Kris. He has years of experience with people who want him to leave, and he isn't about to cave so easily to some disembodied guy who won't even show his face. The next room is just as empty, and he eyes one of three doors, straight ahead. The other doors are on either side of him, and he hesitates before choosing the door to his right. He shoves it open then steps back, and a tremendous weight hits the floor where a normal man would have already stepped over the threshold. Upon closer examination, it seems to be a heavy stone chair.

"Nice try," Kris tells the air. He steps on and over the chair into the room, and the door shuts behind him, leaving him alone with his torch. A shadow flickers into view, first within the torch, then without; a dark presence seems to touch the back of Kris' neck, and he suppresses a shiver as the room grows darker. His torch extinguishes itself at the same time his eyes adjust enough to see the shadowy figure before him.

"I warned you," the voice says, echoing from the huge shape, that mass of undefined darkness. It's so easy to project his

fear onto it, but Kris holds back, trying to see it for what it is, rather than what Wilson's da told him it would be. *"I warned you to get out. To leave. And you—"*

"Do you have a name?" Kris asks. The shape, still shimmering, falls silent.

"What?" it asks. The coldness, damp and wet along Kris' shoulders, starts to creep down his spine at the question.

"A name," Kris says. "Have you ever had a name?"

The silence fills the room, the shape swelling, then shrinking, then swelling again. *"I have no name."*

"Everyone's got a name," Kris says. "Even demons, or beasts, or whatever it is you are."

Silence again.

"What," the voice asks, *"did you mean, when you said you have to 'clear the castle'?"*

"I was hired to do it," Kris says. "Well, I wasn't paid yet. In case I die, I'm guessing. But The Duke wants to use your castle for something, I suppose, so they sent me to clear you out of it."

"The Duke?" the thing asks. *"The Duke wants my castle? My castle? After all these years?"*

"Guess so," Kris says. "It's your castle, then? You're not just squatting here?"

"No, it's mine," it tells him. Kris nods, reaching into his pocket for another bundle of sticks.

"How long've you lived here?" Kris asks. The thing hums.

"I don't know," it says. *"Time doesn't matter to me."*

"Nah, I get that," Kris says. "I can respect that. You're a monster, I've heard. Monsters probably don't tell time much."

"That's right," it says. Kris lifts his boot, just slightly, and bends a little bit.

"Sounds right," Kris says. "Has anyone tried to clear the castle before?"

"All have failed," it tells him. *"All have run in terror."*

"Anyone die?" Kris asks.

Silence. Kris' skin is warming, drying up. The thing seems to have pulled back, filling only its own space now.

"What?" the thing asks again.

"You kill anyone?" Kris asks. "Anyone ever die here?"

"I've never killed anyone, no," it says. *"And nobody has died here in a very long time."*

"Thought you couldn't tell time," Kris says.

"*It* feels *long,*" the thing clarifies, shimmering, without definition. Just shadows and dread. *"Feels so very, very long."*

All in one fast, striking movement, Kris lights the bundle of kindling on fire and brings the flame to the torch, letting it lick back into life, casting the thing into light for the first time. Kris stares at it, then blinks, his eyes refocusing.

"Oh," Kris says, when he realizes what he's seeing. The room is filled with furniture, nearly seeming lived-in and almost *warm*, even nicer than his cabin. The shadow has shrunk to a shape even smaller than Kris: the shape of a man. "You're just a guy."

The man stares at him, his face gaunt and white, eyes squinted and angry. "I am not *just* anything. I am the occupant of this house, and *you* are a trespasser."

"You certainly are occupying this house," Kris says. "You must have a name. You're a normal guy."

"I am not a *normal guy*," the guy says. He stares at Kris for a beat longer. "But, uhh. My name is Beau."

"Beau?" Kris repeats. "*Your* name is Beau?"

"Yeah," says the guy, apparently named Beau, his brow furrowing. He seems finely built, with delicate features and light bones, looking like he weighs almost nothing. He has on an expensive-looking suit, bespoke albeit quite old, and his long, dark hair is neatly combed back from his face. He doesn't look like any beast Kris has ever heard a story about. "What of it?"

"Nothing," Kris says. He reaches for his sword.

"What are you doing?" Beau demands, taking a step back, arm raised as if he can catch the blade in his bare hand, should Kris choose to swing it.

"Full disclosure," Kris says, unhooking his first scabbard, then the second, letting them clatter to the stone floor. He steps out of his knife belts and let them, too, fall in a circle where his feet had been. He inches forward onto a rug and sheds his coat.

76

"I came ready to drive out a monster, not accidentally kill some guy."

"You couldn't've," Beau tells him. "I'm already dead."

Kris looks up, faintly surprised. "No shit," he says, tugging off his scarf. "Could've fooled me, what with the walking and talking and everything."

"I don't know why I'm like *this,*" Beau says. "But I am dead. I can prove it."

"You can?" Kris says. He readjusts the basket on his back. "Then, by all means."

Beau leads Kris through the next door, and then another, glancing over his shoulder at him periodically like he thinks Kris might either bolt or tackle him to the ground. Kris has no intention of doing either; his day has turned out much more interesting than he had anticipated when he woke up that morning, and the guy seems both handsome and nice, albeit a bit waifish and maybe more than a bit skittish.

"Through here," Beau instructs, after they climb a high set of stone stairs, Kris' boots making the only sounds of footfalls as they walk. He holds open a wooden door and Kris ducks inside the new room, finding himself in a dark bedroom. The huge bed pressed against the far wall seems to take up a lot of the space, with its burgundy hangings and rich brass posts. Beau ghosts past him and to the bedside, silent, his face drawn.

"See?" Beau asks, motioning to the bed. Kris steps up behind him and peers around the curtain he is holding back to find a dusty corpse, mostly-decomposed, primarily made of bone and hair.

"Wow," Kris says. "Yikes."

"Yeah," Beau says softly. "Yikes."

Kris reaches around him and gently smoothes the covers down around the chest of the skeleton. Beau extends his own hand, grasps the skull in his hand, and jerks it upwards, dislodging it from the spine.

"Looks better than I ever did before," Beau jokes lightly. He hefts his own skull in his hand like it's a toy, then hands it off to Kris. Kris takes it, hesitantly; after a moment of inspecting it, he holds it beside Beau's flesh-covered head. He can see the resemblance. "This was you, then?"

"It was," Beau tells him. "Not anymore."

"Looks like it hasn't been for a while," Kris comments. He settles the skull back on the pillow gingerly, suppressing the urge to tuck the grimy bedsheets around the dead thing. "And you don't know why you're a ghost, or whatever it is you are?"

"Nope," Beau tells him, his lips popping a little on the *p*. "I have no idea, and everything I do— Well. I can't seem to leave."

"What, leave forever?" Kris asks, and Beau nods. "You've been given an opportunity here, buddy. You lived past death. I wouldn't waste that so fast."

"It's lonely," Beau snaps. Kris shuts his mouth, and they stare at each other for a long time.

"Yeah?" Kris asks, thinking of his own empty cabin, of the unmarked graves in his backyard, courtesy of the winter of two years' past. He thinks of the town full of people who scowl at him as he passes. He looks down at Beau, then back at the corpse on the bed. "Sucks to be lonely."

"Yes," Beau says. He says that word differently than The Duke's Pissant does, like he knows it better, like he knows the world better.

"I've heard a lot of stories," Kris tells him. Beau glances at him, brow furrowed again. His dark eyes, for how dead he truly appears to be, are blazing. "You know. Legends. About people with unfinished business, and how there are things that can release them. Want me to try one?"

"Sure," Beau says. "Yes, I would like that, thank you."

"Great," Kris says, before taking Beau's head between his hands. He's small, but he feels less delicate like this than his own skull had felt just moments ago. He has a solid weight to him, filled with a warmth that belies his status as a spirit. Kris shifts, then bends down, pressing his lips to Beau's. Beau startles backwards, staring at him, one thin hand over his mouth.

"What?" Beau asks, then frowns. *"What?"* he demands this time. Kris shrugs.

"I read it in a story," Kris says, since that's all the explanation he thinks he needs. Beau glares at him, then shuffles forward a step. "True love's kiss."

"That's awfully presumptuous of you," Beau says.

"Well," Kris says, "I'm lonely, too."

"Are you?" Beau asks. "This place... You know, it's hard, when I'm the only one rattling around it. It's lonely."

"You said that already."

"Did I?"

"You did." Kris shrugs his basket off, letting it drop to the floor. "You know, if I *had* cleared this castle, I was just going to use the money to buy a new house in a new place anyways. If I stay here… Well, that's just as good, I think. Don't you?"

Beau nods, shifting his weight to his other foot, then glances out the window. It's still snowing, but the sun is starting to come up, turning the falling snow orange in the growing light. "Will they come looking for you?"

"Probably," Kris tells him. "But you put on quite the show back there, and I've got a lot of training with my knives. I don't think they'll be clearing the both of us out anytime soon."

"What about The Duke?" Beau asks. Kris looks down at him, and feels an overwhelming urge to smile. He fights it off.

"Fuck the duke," he says, sweeping Beau up in his arms. Beau grins against his mouth, then pulls back.

"Are you sure?" Beau asks. Kris looks out the window, too, at the sunrise, at the snow like thousands — like millions — of tiny flames, falling to the earth in the new dawn sunlight.

"How did you become a ghost?" Kris asks abruptly. Beau glances up at him.

"I don't know," Beau says. "But there are things in this castle. Other things. They told me, when people die here, they have to stay here, like me. I'm *very* careful — nobody dies here. They usually die in the woods or down in the town or something."

"You're *sure* about that?" Kris says. "That if someone dies here, they turn out like you?"

Beau steps back, squares his shoulders, lifts his chin. Looks Kris right in the eye.

"I'm *sure*," Beau says, with the gravity of someone who hasn't had the opportunity to really be *sure* about anything in years.

"Great," Kris tells him. He thinks back to the graves in his backyard, and to the unkind eyes of the villagers in the tavern, and the lonely, heavy feeling that settles over him every night, when he climbs, alone, into a cold bed, in a cold house. He feels his own heart pound in his throat, then settle, like it already knows what he wants and has decided, yes, this is more than okay.

"Got any rope?" Kris asks, when his pulse balances back out.

Beau eyes him, but leads him back out of the room. Kris reaches down and lifts him up, tossing him over his shoulder, and follows his directions through the castle.

"Are you sure?" Beau asks, when they're on top of the castle. The wind whips them in the face; Kris pushes his hair back out of his eyes and focuses on tying the tightest possible knot he can. "What if—"

"What if it doesn't work?" Kris finishes the question before Beau can. "You've asked me that nineteen times. Those cursed spirits following you around seem to think it'll work."

"But if it *doesn't*—"

"If it doesn't, buddy," Kris says, "I'm no worse off than I am right now."

Beau is silent for a long moment, so Kris turns back to look at him. He has a crumpled look on his face, like he is really struggling internally with some sad words he doesn't know how to say.

"Sorry," Kris says. Beau shakes his head.

"No, I get it," Beau replies. "I just wish things were better for you."

Kris looks down at the rope, quadruple-knotted around the highest spire of the castle. He lifts the noose carefully tied into the other end of the rope and holds it in his hands, as if weighing and measuring it.

"Yeah," Kris says. "Me, too." He tightens the knot again. "Hopefully, it's about to be."

Beau does the sign of the cross and Kris lassoes his own neck with the noose. He looks back at Beau, then over the edge, at how far away the ground is if the rope snaps. Optimistically, it won't. With his luck, though? Who knows.

"You're *sure?*" Beau asks again. Kris doesn't sigh, but it's a close thing. He gets the concern, he really does, but things don't matter so much in the village anymore. He's been pretty close to doing this on his own anyways; at least, this way, he potentially gets Beau out of it, and Beau is the best *anything* he's encountered in years.

"Yeah," Kris says, "I'm sure."

Kris steps up onto the edge, and Beau covers one eye with his hand, head half-tilted away. Kris finds a kind of twisted humor in a ghost who can't watch someone die, but the thought cuts off halfway through when the wind shoves him over the edge.

He feels himself falling, falling, the tops of the trees blurring past him in a whiz of green, white, and brown, and then, suddenly, he's standing beside Beau again. Beau startes at him, incredulous.

"Did you jump back up?" Beau asks, shocked. Kris laughs.

"Fuck no," he says. He leans over the edge and sees his own body swinging at the end of the noose, neck clearly snapped. He hopes he didn't shit himself; that would probably be embarrassing. "Fuck, it worked."

"You swear a lot," Beau comments.

"Get used to it, baby," Kris says, turning and sweeping Beau up into his arms. Beau laughs, overjoyed, and lets himself be handled back inside.

When Adrian arrives four days later, the wind howls fiercely, blowing him back several steps down the path. He forces his way forwards, then stops at the front of the castle and looks directly up, at the shape swinging from the highest point of the roof. He squints, and makes out distinctly the hanged corpse of Kris, still huge in death, as it dangles by rope from the castle.

"Shit," Adrian manages to say, before he turns and vomits into the snow. When he glances back up, the corpse is still swinging there, bouncing off the stone facade. Adrian averts his eyes and pushes his way inside. He is instantly engulfed in darkness; the heavy doors swing shut behind him, brass knockers and locks slamming and clicking into place. Adrian turns slowly, carefully, trying to adjust to the blackness.

"*Leave,*" says a voice from the endless shadows, a soft, unfamiliar, disembodied voice. He means to scoff, but a cold blade presses into the hot flesh at his throat at the same moment. He freezes.

"Now," orders a voice he knows well. He tries to turn his head, but sees only shadows looming larger and larger still as the metal digs harder into his skin, drawing blood to trickle down his chest.

"Kristian?" Adrian tries to ask. A vise seems to wrap around his chest, to tighten there, but when he looks down, he sees only tendrils of darkness.

"Don't come back," Kris' voice says. *"Tell them what you saw. Tell them never to come here again."*

The shadows release Adrian, and he glances around, feeling wild. The shadows retreat, then swell when he does not move, surrounding him.

"Go," say both voices together, and Adrian steps back once, then again, then turns tail. He lets the heavy doors bang shut behind him, locking in place once again, and he abandons that place. He can still hear Kris' voice echoing, can still see his

body hanging from the roof, and he sprints back towards the town to warn them.

Back in the castle, Kris locks the front doors, sliding the tremendous bolt into place and turning back around. Beau runs at him, leaping up into his arms and kissing him fiercely.

"Good going," Kris says around his mouth. Beau pulls back and presses his forehead to Kris', beaming from ear-to-ear. "You know, normal guys don't usually do stuff like this."

"Oh, and we're such normal guys," Beau laughs. Kris kisses him again and sets him down.

"Fuck normal guys," Kris says, and Beau high-fives him, still laughing.

BACCHANALIA

Wes rides the high of winning the game for a while after the game actually ends. To stand up before thousands of people, and even more through the television and the radio, and play a game like baseball is an intense and difficult thing. Wes *loves* it. He loves the people shouting for him, the signs with his name on them, the lights and the sounds and the crack of a bat against a ball. He just loves the whole damn thing.

He loves his team, too.

It's not hard to love his team; they're a great group of guys, and they're genuinely his best friends. He spends most of his time outside of the games with them, too. They all like hanging out, they all have the same job (obviously), they all have similar hobbies. It's all great.

Once the game is over, Wes goes back to the dugout. Clarence holds a hand out to him to shake, and when he does,

Clarence's index finger lightly scratches his palm. When Clarence pulls back, he gives Wes a meaningful look. Wes moves to give Allen the same handshake.

The team gets showered and changed and everyone heads out separately to the parking lot, still happy, still fooling around with each other after their great win. Clarence makes eye contact with him over the hood of his red Chevy, and everyone is, momentarily, silent. They all climb into their cars and follow Clarence as he drives out of the lot and down the road.

Chicago is far from empty this late at night, but it is dark. The street lights and bright signs are too artificial to feel like real light, and Wes is having an out-of-body experience, feeling like he's travelling through space as he follows Wes to the edge of the city and out, towards the suburbs. There's a beautiful patch of woods they frequent that will do perfectly for tonight.

Clarence navigates them all towards parking in a clearing, and they do, lined up flawlessly underneath the trees. They all climb out of their vehicles, and some of Wes' teammates start digging through their trunks. Leon pulls out their masks. Eddie has their torches. Allen has a cooler filled with grapes and wine. Ray has their drums. Eugene has the knives.

Leon brings the bull-head mask to Clarence, and Clarence strips off his shirt before he slides the head on. He turns to the rest of them, all illuminated in the headlights of their cars.

"Light the torches," Clarence says. His voice is slightly muffled, but they can all still hear him clearly. "Turn off your cars. Ray, set up your drums, start playing once you're ready."

Everybody does as they've been told to do. Ray gets his drums organized and slides his mask into place before starting to slam on the animal skins stretched across the tops of his instruments. The heavy percussion fills the woods as everyone puts their masks on and lights torches. The flames flicker and fire lights the clearing better than the headlights ever could, and so everyone shuts off their lights and their cars and stands in the dancing shadows.

"First, the performance," Clarence shouts over the drums. Eddie and Walter go to the center of the clearing to start the dance they always do. Allen starts passing out wine as they begin their dramatic performances. They've been doing these festal processions and dramatic performances and praises sent skyward for long enough that it all falls into place so easily.

"The Anthesteria," Clarence announces. Eddie and Walter's dance starts slowing as Allen hands out the last jug of wine. "Allen. The Oschophoria."

Allen carries the grape clusters to Clarence and stuffs them into the mouth of the bull's head. Clarence yanks them into the head and swallows them that way as Wes watches from behind his own mask. It's hard to see in the firelight, but he's seen it so many times, it's nothing special now. It's the rush of it that really gets him.

Everyone is still wearing their uniform pants, but nobody has shirts on. Just barefoot in their grass-stained trousers, grape juice and skins smeared like paint across their bare chests, and masks on every face in the bunch. The dichotomy between the pants and the primal skins, the contrast, brings goosebumps to Wes' arms. The hair on the back of his neck stands up. He *loves* it.

The Lenaea is finished. The shows have stopped. The drinking feast has begun. Clarence lifts his jug and calls, "Begin the rites."

The Rite of Bacchus. When Clarence had first gotten them all into doing this, he had saved telling them about the Rite of Bacchus for last. It's a simple, old-fashioned rite, and one of many, and it has three stages.

The first stage is death.

"To death," Clarence shouts. The drums beat slightly faster, and he holds his jug in the air, high above his bull-head. Everyone else on the team lifts their jugs, as well, and they start drinking the wine. There's more to the wine than just grapes and honey, Wes knows that. He just doesn't know *what* else is in it. He assumes some sort of drug, but he doesn't know what, exactly, or why it's given to them. He drinks it all anyways. He's part of the team.

"Enter the underworld," Clarence calls. The drums feel like they're distorting, like they're both speeding up and slowing down. Wes stares out of his deer mask at the people around him. Their heads meld with their masks until they have animal heads and the bodies of men. It's disorienting but familiar, and Wes can feel tears streaming down his face. The alcohol and whatever else is in it is working.

Ralph goes back to his car and pulls out a bow and arrows. He is the best hunter of all of them. He jogs towards the trees at the edge of the clearing and slips into them, Allen and Eugene following behind to help him if he finds an animal. The drums speed up, and Wes keeps drinking from his jug. It has his name carved into the side; beneath it, there's a roughly-drawn crescent moon.

"I've done it!" Ralph calls from the woods. It feels like he's been gone for two seconds and two hours. He and Eugene haul a deer into the center of the clearing, Allen bringing up the rear, carrying Ralph's bow. The deer bleeds from the arrow wound in his neck, the arrow still protruding there. They drop him to the ground, and Wes is among the men who surge forward. One of their rituals is just this omophagic feast, pulling a live animal to pieces and eating them raw.

"This is the death and rebirth of Bacchus," Clarence calls over the drums and the sounds of tearing flesh. Chicago seems so far away in these moments. The drums sound just like the roaring crowds who scream every time he slams a ball out of the park with his bat. His teammates crowd around him like they do when they win a game after being behind for eight innings. He's joyous, overjoyed even. There is so much to have here, so much to be, and it's so easy to let go of everything outside of this moment.

"Become one with Bacchus," Clarence shouts. This is the enthusiasm. This is the next step of their rites. This is when they let Bacchus enter their bodies. This is the infant death and rebirth of the god.

Once the deer has been consumed, the men leave the bones to finish stripping one another. Wes drinks from his wine

jug again and lets Ralph yank his baseball trousers off as he does.
Allen digs the cymbals out of Ray's car and slams on them while
Ray continues playing the drums. There are screams, but Wes
doesn't know who they're from. The cymbals and drums drown
them out. Someone bites Wes' shoulder. He thinks it might be
Walter.

Then, there's a sound in the woods. The crack of a
branch, and it seems louder than it would normally, but the
drums and cymbals stop and the screaming stops and the men all
stop. Wes is among the first men to move, and he, Leon, and
Clarence head for the woods where they heard the snap. It's
deadly silent as they do, silent enough to hear each man's heavy
breathing as they trek through the trees, searching for the source
of the sound.

Wes sees a shadow move.

"There," he shouts. His deer mask muffles his voice, but
Clarence and Leon both jog to him and they sprint off after the
shadow. Wes moves the fastest; faster than Clarence the bull,
faster than Leon the raven. Wes leaps from the ground and

tackles the shadow to the dirt, pinning himself against its shoulders.

"It's a man," Wes calls backwards. He hauls the man up by his shirt.

"What the fuck is this?" the guy asks. "Who the fuck are you?"

"It's a *man*," Clarence echoes. He takes over from Wes, dragging the guy back into the clearing with the rest of the team. "It was a man!"

There's a roar of cheers and shrieks and screams, and the drums and cymbals pick up again. The man is saying something, looking directly into Wes' eyes as he pleads for— *something*, Wes has no idea what. He keeps repeating something, over and over, but Wes can't understand it. It's like he's not speaking a human language, or Wes can't understand human languages.

Wes is the first one to grab him. This is the final step of the night. They're lucky they found him so easily; sometimes they just stumble in like this, but sometimes they need to be hunted. Wes pushes the man down next to the bones of the deer. The drums speed up, and the cymbals clang and crash. Wes' head is filled with sounds and screams and the animalistic understanding of a deer, and nothing else. He pins the man to the ground, takes the blade offered to him, and does to him what he did to the deer earlier that night. The team surges around him. Wes relishes in it.

The World Series is coming up, so emotions are running high. The games are tense and colors are bright and sounds are loud. Wes cracks a grand slam out of the park towards the end of the game and his teammates surge around him. Someone grabs him around the neck, and the bite mark on his shoulder still smarts.

"That was such a goddamn *hit*, Wes, my God," Leon shouts to him. Wes turns his head and Clarence is looking at him, grinning. He points at his shoulder, and Wes tugs his jersey up a little further to cover himself up. Between the cheers of the crowd and the blurring of his teammates around him and the piercing vibrance of the lights during this night game, Wes swears he can hear drums and cymbals.

THE SPIRIT OF FEAR

"How very little can be done under the spirit of fear."

Florence Nightingale

The sunset in El Jadida paints the sky in magnificent colors. Leah sits on the edge of a walkway that separates the land of Morocco and its bright cityscape from the black, roiling sea below. Her legs dangle into the empty air. She feels the cooling stone beneath her hands, a grounding presence after the day she's had.

Her phone rings.

She looks out at the sunset for one last, long moment before she digs her phone from her pocket, swipes to answer the call, and lifts it to her ear. "This is Nightingale."

"Hi," a high, shaky voice says on the other end. "I— Someone gave me your card. In a restaurant. In Bismarck. They should I said— I'm sorry, I mean, they said I should call you. When my husband wasn't home."

"What's your husband's name?" Leah asks. She leans back on one hand, watching the horizon in the distance as the sun drops down.

"Daniel Robert Rose," the voice says, after a moment of hesitation.

"And where do you live?" Leah asks. There's another long pause. Leah waits it out.

"Redwater, North Dakota," the woman tells her.

"Do you want him dead?" Leah asks. It's easiest to just be blunt and let them decide how serious they are. Usually, the answer is very. Leah still doesn't make assumptions.

There's less of a pause this time. "Yes," the woman whispers. Leah nods.

"I'll do it," Leah says. "Be safe."

"Thank you," the woman tells her. "Be careful. He's got a lot of friends."

"I can handle them," Leah says, before she hangs up. She looks out at the sunset for a little while longer, before the sun dips completely into the ocean and the sky goes blue and black, blending in with the sea. She heaves herself to her feet, then, and turns, leaving El Jadida behind her.

———

Redwater, North Dakota is more than it seems, which Leah never would have guessed before she actually ended up there. She stands outside a crumbling church in the center of town and looks around, and nothing catches her attention. It's the overwhelming *amount* of nothingness, however, that's setting her on high alert. There should be *somebody* out, even if it's just a street-cleaner or a shopkeeper or something like that.

It's only eight o'clock, and Redwater is empty.

Leah did her research before showing up in town, and she knows exactly where Daniel Rose lives. She walks there, casually, from the center of town. There's mostly back roads, but it's a really tiny town, so she just keeps her hands in her pockets and walks the distance. Still, nobody seems to be here. The houses don't seem to have life in them; the windows are all dark.

Eventually, she reaches the home of the Roses — Daniel, plus his wife, Audrey, and their daughter, Sabrina. It's the same here that it is everywhere else: lights off, no signs of life, no indication that anybody actually lives in this godforsaken town. Leah lights up a cigarette and stares at the house from the sidewalk. Smoke trails up to the sky, and she walks up to the front door. She knocks.

The door opens almost immediately.

Leah's been doing this long enough not to be startled, but she is slightly surprised that the door is answered so quickly. She looks down at a small blonde child, and the child looks back up at her. Sabrina.

"Nobody should be out past six," Sabrina tells her firmly. "Especially not a lady."

"Is that why there's nobody outside?" Leah asks. "There's a curfew?"

"Yes," Sabrina says.

"Is your daddy home?" Leah asks. Sabrina looks over her shoulder. "Hey, sweetheart. It's okay. Just tell me if he's home. Nod your head for yes, shake it for no."

Sabrina eyes her, silent, unmoving.

"Your mommy called me," Leah says. Sabrina keeps looking at her.

"Dad has a lot of friends," Sabrina tells her. "You can't stop them."

Leah frowns, just a little, eyebrows pulling together as she studies this little girl. "Are they hurting you?"

Sabrina looks over her shoulder again. "No."

"Hey," Leah says. Sabrina looks back at her. "It's okay. You can tell me if they are. I can stop it."

Sabrina stares at Leah, a long, hard stare, unbreaking. Eventually, she nods, almost imperceptibly.

"And is he home?" Leah asks. Sabrina nods again, just a little upwards twitch of her head. Leah nods back. "Can I come in?"

"Please be quiet," Sabrina tells her, but she backs out of the way to allow Leah inside. Leah goes, drawing her pistol as she moves silently into Sabrina's darkened home. She can't see anyone except Sabrina, but the little girl points deeper into the house. Leah goes, follows the direction she points in. Sabrina doesn't go with her, which is probably for the best.

The house is pitch-black, but Leah can hear rustling, far away, deep inside of the house, so she just follows that. She takes it all one step at a time, moving gingerly, careful not to trip over anything or make any noise. She successfully makes it to a dark kitchen, and hears a sound behind what she can only assume is a pantry door. She comes up on the door, silently, and edges it open — and there's a woman inside.

"Please," the woman says, empty hands up in front of her face, shaking. Her voice is familiar: it's Audrey Rose. "He knows you're here. He went into the basement."

"Which way is that?" Leah asks. The woman points, and Leah goes. She finds a door along the far wall of the kitchen and opens it, and it does indeed have stairs leading down into a basement. She goes down one step, slowly; it doesn't creak. She takes the next step, then the next, each step down into the basement until she's standing on the hard stone floor. She listens, stock-still, silent. A rustle. She turns, follows the sound, and suddenly there's the blast of gunfire, a shot going off and missing her head by a foot.

Ears ringing, Leah calculates her shot and fires at her attacker's knee. Based on the pained groan and the thud of a body hitting the floor, she hit her target. She digs a flashlight from her pocket and shines it on the ground, and finds the man's face. She knows him; she found his photo time and time again during her research. This is Daniel Rose.

"You can't kill me, you fucking cunt," is the last thing Daniel Rose says before Leah shoots him through the forehead. He slams back into the ground and slumps into a dead heap, and Leah steps over him, crouching to check his pulse. Nothing in his throat, nothing in his wrists, no breath in what's left of his mouth and nose. She leaves him there, jogs back upstairs and to the pantry.

"It's done," Leah says, and Audrey comes flying out of the pantry, slamming into her, wrapping her up into an embrace.

"Bree! Come out here!" Audrey calls, and Sabrina comes running. She wraps herself around her mother's legs, sobbing. Audrey turns from Leah to crouch and hold her daughter.

"I should leave now," Leah says.

"No!" Sabrina shouts. "No, they're going to know it was you—"

"Baby, shush," Audrey whispers to Sabrina. Leah frowns at them.

"What do you mean?" Leah asks. "Who is 'they'?"

Audrey looks down at Sabrina for a long, long time. Leah knows the expression of someone who's deciding whether or not they're about to make the right decision, so she waits. Eventually, Audrey says, "The men in this town... I don't know how to explain it."

"They're mean to us," Sabrina says.

"That's explanation enough for me," Leah tells her. "Mean like your dad was?"

"Yes," Sabrina says. Audrey's eyes shut when Leah says *was*. "Jodie's dad is mean to her, too. And Jenny's. And Heidi's—"

"They have some strange ideas," Audrey interrupts. "They just…"

When nothing else seems forthcoming, Leah asks, "Do they hurt you?"

"Yes," Audrey says. Sabrina nods in agreement.

"They killed Dolly," Sabrina says.

"Who was Dolly?" Leah asks.

Audrey looks out the window. "She lived next door. Danny and Jason and them killed her a couple of months ago.

She was... Well, Danny said she was acting up. I didn't think— I don't know. Maybe she was."

"Even if she was, she doesn't deserve to die," Leah says. She checks her pistol again. "Is this every man in town?"

"Almost," Audrey says. "The boys aren't so bad. We're trying to help them."

"Men only," Leah says. "Got it."

She goes out the back door, into the backyard, and scales the picket fence into the next yard, where Audrey had glanced while talking about Dolly. The house is similarly dark, but she knows that that doesn't mean anything anymore. There's a teenage girl and a little boy inside the kitchen when she breaks in through the window.

"My father's downstairs," the girl says. The house has a similar layout to Audrey's, and Leah goes down the basement steps into their stone basement. She hears a creak, and then the basement door to the backyard opens up. Leah fires and catches him in the back, knocking him onto the dirty steps. She goes to him.

"What's your name?" Leah asks.

"Fuck you," the man spits. "She deserved it."

Leah fires a shot into the back of his head. He stops moving.

"No, she didn't," Leah says. She checks his pulse; he's dead, too. She returns upstairs to find that Audrey and Sabrina have come over and are speaking in low tones with the teenager and her younger brother.

"We want to help," Sabrina says, as soon as Leah's within her line of sight. All four of them look at her.

"Help with what?" Leah asks.

"We want to kill the others," the teenager says. "The rest of them. All the men in town."

"Please," the little boy says. Leah looks them all over. They seem helplessly, hopelessly earnest, desperate in that way you can only be when you have nothing to lose and everything to gain.

"I don't need help," Leah tells them. Audrey shakes her head.

"We need it," Audrey says. "It's for us to do. We have to. We just want you to— to show us. To help us. Please."

Leah stares at them. She deliberates. Then, she turns to the teenager. "What's your name?"

"Sam," she says.

"And yours?" Leah asks the little boy.

"Andy," he says. Leah nods to them, then glances out the window.

"How many people are in this town?" Leah asks. The children look to Audrey.

"In our village, there's only about eighty-two," Audrey says. "We're small. There's about twenty-one other men, besides Danny and Jason."

"Is Jason the one—" Leah starts to ask, then stops. She points downstairs, and Audrey nods. "Alright. Is everyone on your side? Have you discussed this?"

"We've discussed it," Audrey tells her. "We've never been able to plan it."

Leah nods. She looks out the window again at the darkened town. She can see a couple of streets from her vantage point; everything is dark in this impossibly small prison of a town.

"Do you have a phone tree or something?" Leah asks. Audrey nods. "Call everyone. Call all the women and children.

Do you have a place we can meet? Can they get out of their houses?"

"The men already know," Audrey says. "They always know."

"Tell them to be safe, but to meet us at your house," Leah says. "We'll give them until midnight. If anyone can't get out, we'll go to them first. Tell them that. Okay?"

"Okay," Audrey tells her, and runs for the phone on the kitchen wall. Sabrina and Andy follow her, but Sam just stands there, looking at Leah.

"We should start with the sheriff," Sam says. "His daughter's name is Katie. She's almost nineteen and she can take over after he's done."

"Perfect," Leah tells her. She jerks her chin in the direction of the knife block on the kitchen counter. "Arm yourself. We'll start there."

Things go as smoothly as they can to prepare. Audrey starts her phone tree, calls everyone she knows and tells them to tell everyone else, even if they might already know, just to be sure, just to be *absolutely certain*. Leah watches her make phone calls as she pulls all the weapons she has off of her person and passes them out amongst her little group.

"You have to be quick," Leah tells the children. "They're going to try and stall. They're going to talk to you. They're trying to trick you. You can't let them."

"Okay," all three of them say at once. They each have knives. Audrey gets Leah's second pistol. They go back next door, back to Audrey's house, and find a couple of women already outside. Over the next couple of hours, most of the women and children of the town show up, and they're all seated silently in Audrey's living room. A couple of them talk softly amongst themselves, and the younger children are pleasantly distracting as they play near the cold fireplace, but otherwise the room is chillingly still.

"Does everybody have a weapon?" Leah asks of the twenty-four women in the living room. There's five women who couldn't make it, and Leah's already mapped out with Audrey to stop at their homes first to pick them up along the way. The town has thirty children, and twenty-three of them are in the room. Leah already knows who is where. They have a route. They have a plan. This is Leah's job, and it is these women's last chance of salvation.

"Yes," the women reply. Audrey stands at Leah's right hand, pistol weighing heavy in her palm. They lead the women and children from the home down the street, to the sheriff's house. The sheriff is waiting for them, and fires at their feet, but Leah can see him in the window, and she aims to kill. Katie, the sheriff's daughter, comes sprinting outside, arms full of weapons, and distributes them to the women who volunteer as marksmen.

The five women who need to be freed are let go first. They don't go without a fight, and Elizabeth, one of the college-aged women in the group, takes a gunshot to the shoulder. A nurse stops her and tends to her wound while the rest of them go on.

The women have barely any love lost on these men. They rescue their friends and carry their children and pick off the men of the town one by one. It's obvious, at least to Leah, that some of them have been waiting a long time for this.

The last house is by far the most dangerous, and the most difficult; he's got a bunker, ready for the apocalypse. Everyone in town is wary of him, and so they approach the house from all sides, surrounding him.

"Archie!" Laverne, his wife, calls to the house. "Archie, come out!"

There's no answer from the house. Laverne looks over her shoulder and Leah, and Leah shakes her head. *Not yet.*

"Archie, please!" Laverne shouts at the house. Still nothing. "If you come out, it'll all be okay!"

It won't be. She's lying. He's the last man in town. The crowd has grown; there are thirty children, twenty-nine women, and Leah, and all of them are armed. The teenage boys look lighter, freer; the young children are smiling. The women have creased faces and hunched backs and they're finally safe.

"Fuck off!" a man's voice calls from inside the house. It can only be Archie.

"He has a stockpile in there," Laverne tells Leah. "Guns, gunpowder, grenades, the whole nine. What do we do?"

"He's the only one in there," Leah says. "Let him blow it up if he wants."

Laverne looks at her home for a little while, then nods. Leah walks up to the front door and knocks.

"Archie," Leah calls. "You wanna come out, big guy? Laverne wants to talk to you."

"Fuck you," Archie spits back. Leah shrugs.

"Fine by me," she says. She turns to the crowd. "Everyone, back up! I want you behind the tree line!"

The group obeys, running to take cover. Leah punches a hole through the window beside the door. Then, she pulls a lighter from her boot and flips the top open.

"Fuck you, too, Archie," Leah says, flicking the lighter on and tossing it through the broken window. She sprints for the crowd, diving when she hears the explosion start, and there are hands on her arms and shoulders pulling her behind the trees, pulling her to safety. When she gets her feet under her and turns, the house is blazing, a column of black smoke rising into the night sky. Everyone stares at it quietly, for a long time, before a sob breaks through the silence.

"We fucking did it!" one of the preteen boys screams, and then the children are cheering and crying and shrieking, clutching each other, running to their mothers. Leah watches them all slam into each other, tears running down smiling faces, young and old finally free. It's a lot to see. She takes a step back, away from the crowd, but then a hand wraps around her wrist and she stops.

"Thank you," Audrey says. She opens her arms, and Leah's not entirely sure what to do, so she lets Audrey hug her. "I just— This is your job? This is what you do?"

Leah half-shrugs as Audrey releases her. "Usually not on this scale, I've never really… seen anything quite like this, to be honest with you."

"They deserved it," Audrey says, cold, and Leah believes her. "But some of the other girls and I— We want to help. We want to do it, too."

"I don't usually… I don't need help," Leah says. "It's just me."

"It doesn't have to be," Sabrina says, appearing at Audrey's side. "We want to help. We can like… work for you?"

Leah stares down at her. When she looks up, all eyes are on her. She turns, and turns, but everywhere she looks, the women and children are looking right at her, expectant, waiting for her to speak. Waiting for her to allow them to join her.

"I don't know," Leah tells them. "Is this something you'd be able to do?"

"What else would we do?" Katie, the sheriff's daughter, asks. "This is what we have. We have a village of fifty-nine people who want to help you."

"Do you have a job description?" one of the woman shouts, and a few people laugh.

"I have business cards," Leah says, and a few more people laugh. "Maybe… I mean, *maybe*. We can train you up. It would help me be in more places at once." She looks them all over. "My avenging hamlet."

"We can all be Nightingale," Sam suggests. "All of us. Everyone will know. They'll fear us."

"We'll never be afraid again," Sabrina says.

"Never," Audrey repeats. She smiles at Leah, and Leah finds herself smiling back.

"Never," Leah agrees. She lets Audrey hug her again, lets the women absorb her into their numbers, lets their voices and hands and warmth wash over her at once.

A EULOGY FOR
HELL'S NEWEST ARRIVAL

Hello, darling husband!

Oh, this?

I just wear it when I don't care what I look like.

It's the same color as your eyes.

It doesn't fit right,

but I like it anyways, I think.

I have a secret to tell you:

Labor Day was two weeks ago

but white satin looks so good on me

that I can't bring myself to care.

Do you care?

Oh, you don't?

How wonderful!

Your willow tree grows nicely when it has fertilizer.

Your backyard is a lush green paradise

when you're not here to guard it.

Thanks for everything you gave me,

especially your mother's candlestick from the mantle,

which I had to throw, still covered in gore, in the trash,

~~down the block,~~

to keep from being recognized.

I appreciate it!

Sorry I don't follow your rules

(I wear white,

I sing loud,

I smash glasses,

fuck you),

but you're not even here to enforce them —

So, I whisper to you,

from six feet away,

"Nice try, buddy;
but I look amazing today
and you can't stop me."

GO ABOUT IN MY LIKENESS

Dame Kitty Beauregarde has been in control of Louisiana since the land was named *La Louisiane* under the Sun King, Louis XIV, whom she never liked all that much. Sure, he was popular, and he sure was handsome, but Kitty never cared much for men who thought too well of themselves. She was there for Louisiana's change from French to Spanish, and back to French, another one of Napoleon's dirty little secrets. Napoleon, too, thought well of himself, and had even less reason to do so. Kitty was happy when he sold the land to America, and she lived in the new Territory of Orleans. Her land has officially changed hands time and time again, but it's always been *hers,* ever since she first stepped foot onto it in 1682.

Kitty has lived on this land for one hundred and thirty-nine years. It is 1821, and she still rules as the queen of the lands. She's been called a queen, a witch, a hag, a demon, a dame, a pythoness, a monarch, a goddess. She likes to tell people that all are true. She took on *dame* as her title; it sounded the most like the French she loves to hear at home.

Louisiana looks different than it did so many years ago, but Kitty likes change. She loves meeting new people, having fresh blood filtering through her woods and bayous. She likes the new sorts of people that keep coming through and asking to stay on her land. Nobody takes advantage of Kitty Beauregarde, not since she put her spell over the land in the late 1600s — a while ago, now.

"Could do with a refresher," Kitty muses to herself. She lives in a tremendous house on the water — literally, *on* the water. She has been a witch for a *very* long time. Her home is entirely safe from the swamp; she learned that trick an absurdly long time ago, now. She enjoys sitting on the colossal wrap around porch, rocking in her wooden rocking chair, watching the people and the animals living around her.

"What was that?" Babette asks, from her rocking chair beside her. Babette is one of Kitty's many daughters. Some of Kitty's daughters are hers, from her womb; some have been taken in by her after leaving their old lives behind. All are equally loved by Kitty. Babette is the closest to Kitty, and adores spending time with her mother.

"I was just thinking how I should recharge the loyalty spell," Kitty tells her. Babette leans over, takes Kitty's hand in hers.

"I'll help you," Babette says. "The Lafayette girls will be here tonight They'd probably love to help, too."

"Of course," Kitty replies. "Is Dominique coming? She's always done well with faith spells."

"She always comes," Babette tells her. She strokes the scarred back of Kitty's hand, then turns her head. Babette has excellent hearing. "Somebody's come to visit you, Mother."

"Who is it?" Kitty asks. Babette releases her hand and stands, leaving Kitty on the porch and vanishing inside the house. Kitty keeps rocking, looking out over the bayou waters. One of those singing toads leaps into the water, sending ripples to the shores, lapping against the trees and the foundations of her home. Kitty shuts her eyes and listens to the insects and the birds, the movement of water, the chirping of crickets.

"Rusty's here to see you," Babette calls. Kitty can hear her moving on light, bare feet back out to the porch; Rusty follows behind in the whisper of flat slippers. She's always dressed well for her station.

"Rusty Frère or Rusty Montagnac?" Kitty asks.

"Montagnac, ma'am," Rusty says softly, in that way she has of speaking like she's a delicate thing. Kitty opens her eyes and looks at the girl. Rusty looks and acts like she's wispy and fragile, a gauzy child made of air, but she's one of the most powerful witches Kitty has ever met. She holds out her hand to Rusty.

"I heard you want to get married," Kitty says. Rusty steps forward and takes Kitty's hand, pressing her lips to the back of it.

Kitty cups Rusty's face in her palm and rubs her thumb under Rusty's bright blue eye.

"I do," Rusty tells her. "He's so handsome, Miss Kitty. I love him so much."

"This is Armand?" Kitty asks. She motions for Rusty to sit in the chair on her other side, and Rusty takes the seat. Babette reclaims her seat on Kitty's left.

"Yes," Rusty says. "Ari. He's been wonderfully good to me. He's been courting me for a while now, and his mother and father adore me. I adore them, too. The whole family is lovely. He has three sisters who welcome me as one of their own."

"This sounds delightful," Babette comments.

"Delightful," Kitty agrees. "Have you come to announce your marriage?"

Rusty looks away, out over the water. Her face is ruddy, and her blue eyes well up with tears, instantly glassy. Kitty reaches over and takes her hand. Rusty laughs without humor, wiping at her face with her other hand.

"I'm so sorry," Rusty whispers. "I just— Yes and no," she answers. "We are to be married. Or, we were."

"What happened?" Kitty asks. Babette rushes into the house and returns with a bit of water in a small glass for Rusty to drink.

"He's died," Rusty tells them. Babette drops the glass, sending it clattering across the porch. She scrambles for it while Kitty squeezes Rusty's hand.

"Darling, I'm so sorry," Kitty says. "I know how you adored him."

"I still do," Rusty says. "I still love him." She looks to Kitty. She has tears in her eyes still, but also a hardened resolve. "I'm not going to let him go. That's why I'm here."

Kitty looks her over. She wonders what this girl might ask of her. Kitty is the most powerful witch anywhere nearby, possibly in the entire South. The look on Rusty's face says she'll do whatever she has to do for this boy.

"What do you want me to do?" Kitty asks. Rusty squeezes her hand, presses the back of Kitty's hand to her mouth and exhales shakily.

"Bring him back," Rusty whispers. "Help me bring him back."

"That's far too risky and you *know* it is," Kitty tells her. "Do you not remember what happened when Clementine tried to bring Adele back? Adele just wasn't the same. It's such a dangerous magic."

"Clementine didn't come to you for help," Rusty tells her. "You can do anything, Miss Kitty. Absolutely *anything*. I *know* you can. I wouldn't dare try without asking for your help first."

Kitty assesses Rusty again. The way she says things, the way she does things: she's always been more powerful than she lets on, but not powerful enough for this. Nobody is powerful enough for this on their own.

"You would do this regardless," Kitty says. Rusty nods.

"I wanted to ask for your help," Rusty tells her, "but I won't hesitate to do it without you if you say no." Rusty watches Babette as she takes her seat again, mopping at her forehead with her kerchief. "I have to do this. I will do *anything* to save Armand."

"Rusty," Babette says to her. "This is so dangerous."

"I would rather die than live without him," Rusty says, in the way of so many before her. Kitty understands; there are a great many people she would rather die than live without. She would never do so, but she understands the desire.

"I will help," Kitty tells her. Rusty shuts her eyes, tears rolling down her cheeks. "If this goes poorly, Rusty, I need to know that you are prepared to do whatever you must to fix what is broken. Do you understand me?"

"Yes," Rusty whispers to her. "I'll do it." They both know what *it* is; *it* means to kill Armand again, if this doesn't work. If he comes back as Adele did, a monster, nothing like her own self, nothing like a human.

"Where is he?" Kitty asks. Rusty stands.

"He is at home with his parents," Rusty says. "I need help to bring him here."

"Babette," Kitty says. Babette stands, as well. "When were the Lafayette girls meant to arrive?"

"Around dusk," Babette tells her. Kitty nods, looking up at Rusty's set jaw. Her expansive strawberry-blonde curls and wide-brimmed hat can't hide a face determined to cross the boundaries between God and man.

"Take Rusty to eat something," Kitty instructs Babette. "When the Lafayette girls come, take half with you. Retrieve the boy's body. Bring him back here once the sun sets. Do not let *anyone* see you, do you understand?"

"Yes, Mama," Babette says. "What shall the other half of the girls do?"

"I need them to collect things for me," Kitty tells her. "Fresh bread, for one. I want yew, yarrow, carnations, gardenias. Frankincense, sandalwood, wormwood, sweetgrass. Heather, certainly. Anise. Amaranth. Dittany of Crete. Pipsissewa, balm of gilead, and asafoetida. Willow bark and lavender. Twelve birds."

"Is that all?" Babette asks. Kitty nods, and Babette inclines her head, taking Rusty by the hand and leading her back inside. She can hear the two young women speaking to each other in low tones inside her home, but she just shuts her eyes and gives them their privacy. They're young; they have so much to talk about.

———

The Lafayette girls show up at dusk, as promised. They're only meant to visit, but when Babette and Rusty relay their night's mission to them, they're happy to help. Kitty listens to them all buzzing around the home, half of them preparing for the

137

journey into the city, the other half preparing for the ritual. Kitty has been resting for the last several hours as Babette calmed Rusty down and made her ready for the night ahead.

Kitty is half-asleep when Rusty comes to her, laying her hand against Kitty's pockmarked forehead. Kitty opens her eyes.

"We will be back soon with Armand," Rusty tells her softly. Kitty reaches up and runs her fingers through the rose-gold of Rusty's auburn hair.

"Be careful," Kitty tells her. Rusty nods to her, and leaves with Babette and half the Lafayette girls. The girls left behind come out onto the porch and stand before Kitty's rocking chair, awaiting instruction.

"We're going to be doing this in the bog," Kitty tells them. The girls all nod. There's about six of them, all told. The other six are with Babette and Rusty. "Create a circle of tranquility and place the birds in it. Start burning the materials I had you gather. Draw necromancy symbols into the water. They don't need to stay; they just need to be drawn on the surface."

"Yes, Dame Beauregarde," most of the girls say, running off to do as she's said. One of the girls lingers for a moment.

"Yes, dear?" Kitty asks. The girl wavers for a moment. Her name is Lisette; Kitty remembers when she was born.

"I'm frightened," Lisette tells her. Kitty nods and sits up slightly, reaching out for the girl. Lisette goes to her, curling into Kitty's lap. Kitty strokes her dark hair back from her face.

"I will protect you," Kitty says. "I will never let anything happen to any of you. Do you hear me?"

"Yes," Lisette tells her. She stays for a moment before she rubs at her face and stands, laughing sheepishly. "I'm sorry, I must seem so foolish."

"It would be foolish not to be afraid," Kitty says. "This is very powerful, old, dark magic we're invoking tonight. I'm afraid, too."

"Don't be," Lisette says. "We'll keep you safe, too."

Kitty nods, and Lisette smiles at her before running off to join her sisters. Kitty looks out over the waters as the girls wade in, flowers and dead birds and bark in hand. They light small fires and trace smoke symbols into the surface of the water as Kitty watches. They're well-prepared; they've been studying all magic, just as Kitty's told them all to do. Perfect, perfect girls.

They stand in the water, holding hands, lighting petals on fire, wringing the blood out of the birds, for some time before Babette and Rusty return with the other sisters and the corpse of Armand. The horse and carriage can be heard on the land, as Kitty and the girls are all quite silent, and the bayou and woods around them have fallen quiet, as well, out of deference to their tasks.

Babette is the first through the back door. She's guiding Rusty, who is helping the other girls carry the coffin. Rusty has tears streaming down her face, but she still stands strong as she bears the body of her most beloved.

"This way," Kitty tells them. She takes them down the stairs to the water and makes them deposit the coffin on the last step. They lift the lid together. He is wrapped inside like a mummy. Rusty unwraps the bandages around his head, and they look down together into the face of Armand.

"How did he die?" Kitty asks. Rusty can't stop staring at Armand's bloodless face.

"We don't know," Rusty tells her. "It came on so suddenly. I can't imagine what it could have been. The physicians were stumped, too."

Kitty looks over his face. There are no obvious signs of trauma, infection, or disease. It is strange that he's been wrapped like this, but Kitty is a bit out of touch with whatever people do with corpses nowadays.

"I've kept him preserved," Rusty tells her. "He's still as good as the day he died."

"Then we haven't got any time to waste." Kitty motions to Armand. "Help me with him."

Between the two of them, they lift Armand from his coffin and into the water. Rusty unwraps him once he's in the water, soaking, revealing his burial suit underneath. They pull him to the Lafayette girls, and, together, they submerge him in the water. The moon rises full and high above their heads, reflecting in the waters between them. A shimmering echo of the moon waves over Armand's dead face.

"Give blood," Kitty instructs. Rusty draws a blade from a holster on her ankle, underneath her wet, heavy skirts. They are up to their waists in water. She drags the knife down her arm and holds the limb over Armand, letting the blood leak into the water. The water is reddened from her blood and the blood of the birds, and smoky from the burning petals and barks. Ash floats with the body.

"I will say the invocation," Kitty says, "and the summoning of his spirit. What you must give is your energy, your intent. When I motion to you, you must say his name. It will bring him back into his body. Do you understand?"

"Yes," Rusty whispers. Kitty puts her hand over Armand's heart, a still, dead thing. It does not beat. Kitty hopes to feel it start again under her fingers, with some of herself; she longs for this to fail with the other half. It's so dangerous, too dangerous.

Kitty knows the invocation and the summons. She recites them perfectly, though she wants to mess them up, just slightly, so he can't come back. She looks to Rusty and her red face and crying eyes, and just can't bring herself to do it. She gives the invocation, and she chants the summons, and she turns to Rusty.

"Speak his name," Kitty says. Rusty looks down at Armand and puts her hand over his face. She smiles. Her eyes look beautiful.

"Satan," Rusty says, so softly, and Kitty can't knock her hand away fast enough. It's too late; Armand's eyes snap open and he starts to stand. It doesn't take long before Armand's body starts to crumble. The spirit of the most powerful of all fallen angels is too much for the body of a mortal man.

"What did you do?" Kitty demands, shielding her eyes from the light blasting through the cracks in Armand.

"I poisoned him," Rusty screams back. "I didn't need him. I needed *magic*. I needed *power.*"

"You had it!" Kitty called to her. She can barely see, can barely hear.

"More," Rusty says. Kitty starts grabbing for the shrieking Lafayette girls as the body of Armand trembles with a barely-contained energy.

"Get underwater!" Kitty shouts to them. The girls all duck underwater, but not Rusty. "Rusty, please!"

"No," Rusty tells her. "I'm finally powerful enough to—"

Kitty ducks underwater before Rusty can finish speaking. She opens her eyes there, in the bayou water, and watches the body of Armand explode. She covers the girl closest to her with her own floating body, keeping her safe there, holding her breath all the while. When the burn goes away, Kitty swims up and breaks the surface of the water. Rusty and Armand are both gone. Three of the Lafayette girls float on the surface of the water, dead. The other nine swim to Kitty, clinging to her. Babette sobs quietly.

Nobody asks questions. Nobody speaks. They all know what Rusty has done. They don't know why. Witches do that, sometimes; his allure is too much to resist, for some. Kitty knows he's not worth it. There is no space for a man like him here on this Earth, or for a woman who would betray her own for him. In the end, they're better than he is. Kitty knows all that. He is an idea. They are real, tangible magic. They are powerful. They have been here for years— decades, centuries, millennia. This is their world.

THE ALIENS HAVE BEEN ASKING ABOUT OUR SPICE ROUTES

"Seth," Marge hisses, waving at her husband's wrist, "put that *down!*"

Seth puts down the fork he has only just picked up. "What's wrong with eating now?" he asks. He pushes his dentures back in his mouth with his hand. Marge bites back a sigh. "Pastor's done talking. We brought the mac and cheese, anyways, so we can eat it whenever we want."

Marge frowns, tucking a strand of white hair behind her ear, and settles her purse back into her lap. "That wasn't your fork," she points out, quietly.

Seth glances at the fork he has just set down, then at the one next to his plate. He looks around the room; the church potluck moves on around him, bustling with all the voices and bodies in the little cafeteria at once, and he apparently considers himself safe to replace his utensil. He nudges the former fork closer to his neighbor's plate. Unfortunately, said neighbor sees the movement and turns to him.

"Seth," says Thomas, Seth's self-proclaimed arch-nemesis, leaning back in his chair. He looks smug, like he's remembering the last Harvest Fair, when his biggest hog beat out Seth's. Seth's face is pinched, like he's remembering the exact same moment. "My man, I didn't notice you there." He claps Seth on the shoulder. "You still on that old farm of yours?"

"Yup," Seth, ever the charmer, says. Marge glares at Thomas.

"Ahh, well," Thomas says. "You'll move on up someday. Take me, for example," Thomas begins to say, but Marge is distracted: Seth is starting to turn a little hazy.

"Honey?" Marge says. Seth turns to her; Thomas scowls.

"I was *talking,*" Thomas says. "I was saying, 'Take me,' and—"

Seth blurs in and out of his chair. Marge blinks at him, then grabs his wrist. The whole of the church cafeteria blinks out of existence, then back in, then out again, before completely blending into darkness. When Marge rubs her eyes, then opens them again, a silver-and-chrome room has replaced the darkness.

"What the heck?" Marge says, turning to find Seth still seated beside her, looking pleasantly confused, but not quite concerned yet.

"Where'd Tom go?" Seth asks. Marge's brow furrows.

"Where'd the *church* go, honey?" Marge says. Seth seems, momentarily, surprised by the unfamiliar room around them. A chime at a door-like apparatus distracts Seth fully, and he gets up off the steel bench they've been transported onto.

"Sit *down*," Marge whispers, but Seth is already walking over to two towering green creatures, offering his hand.

"Pleasure to meetcha," he says, arm still out. The absolute *moron*. He'd say hello to the Devil if he saw him in the cereal aisle. "I'm Seth Bradbury."

The creatures stare down at him with many eyes, examining his body, then his extended arm. They, too, reach out many slithering hands, all of them wrapping around Seth's arm. He shakes, then withdraws, looking only mildly surprised. Marge clutches her purse.

"What can I do for you fellas?" Seth asks. The things stare down at him.

"I am Robert," says one of the monsters. Marge stops being frightened for a moment to be baffled instead. The monster motions to the one beside him. "He is Ted."

"Pleasure," Seth says again. He motions back to Marge. "That's my wife, Marge Bradbury."

"Wife?" Ted asks. Seth spins his hands a little bit. "What is... *wife?*"

150

"Uhh… like, a girl. Mate?" Seth offers. "She gave me kids. I love her a lot."

"We have only male offspring," Ted explains. He motions to Robert. Marge stares at them, dumbfounded. "Robert gave me kids. He took them from Blaison 12."

"Sounds nice," Seth says. "So, what can we do for you folks? I'm guessing you're not from round these parts."

"We are not," Robert says. "We are from Ranawk 6. We came to find a human of high intelligence to communicate with us. We heard a man boasting of his high intelligence, one whom you referred to as… 'Tom.'"

"Oh, Tom!" Seth exclaims, happy. Marge glares daggers at the back of his head, but he keeps talking, still standing in front of the writhing beasts and their many legs. "Yeah, Tom's an alright guy. Not much of a farmer, but he went to college for accounting I think. Was it accounting, baby?"

"No," Marge replies, before she can stop herself. "It was marketing."

"Yeah," Seth says. "Marketing and management."

"Just marketing," Marge says.

"Exactly," Seth agrees, turning back to Robert and Ted. "But he's not the boss at the Grab'n'Go, so I'm not sure what that was for."

"What language is she speaking?" Ted asks, motioning to Marge with seven arms. Seth glances back at her again.

"Uhh," Seth says. "American."

"English," Marge says.

"See, I don't understand that," Robert tells Seth. "What does she have there, anyways?"

"Her purse," Seth says.

"What's it for?"

"Holding things," Seth tells them.

"I have mace in it," Marge says.

"How do you communicate with her if you don't speak the same language?" Ted asks Seth. Seth glances back at Marge, shrugs, and turns to Ted again.

"We manage," Seth says. "To be honest, I never noticed that she spoke English and I spoke American. They sound really alike."

"They don't to us," Robert says. "Regardless. We heard this intelligent human, Tom, assert his own strength of mind, and also request to be taken. We figured, with his advanced intelligence, he must have known we were there, and attempted to take him."

"We took you by accident," Ted adds.

"And your wife by super-accident," Robert continues.

"Sorry," Ted says.

"That's alright," Seth says. "Maybe I can help anyways. Did you need Tom for anything in particular?"

"We wanted a prime example of humanity," Robert says. "The best of the best. Are you a suitable stand-in?"

"Are you sure you don't want Tom?" Marge asks.

"What'd she say?" Robert says, to Seth.

"She asked if you want Tom instead of us," Seth tells them.

"No, we don't have the juice for another beam-up," Ted says. "We only meant to beam up one of you. Two of you took up a lot of energy."

"Do you have enough energy to beam us down?" Marge asks. Robert and Ted both look at Seth.

"She asked if you had the juice to send us home," Seth translates.

"We will shortly," Robert says, "but we do not want to send you home."

"Ahh, well, the kids'll be disappointed," Seth says. Marge reaches, slowly, into her purse, but three of Ted's eyes land on her.

"What's she doing?" Ted demands. Seth glances back at her.

"Oh, she's got snacks in there," Seth tells them, before Marge can tell him to be quiet. "Baby, you got any of those fruit bars in there? The ones Junior likes."

Marge hesitates, then says, "Yeah."

"You'll love em," Seth tells Robert before motioning Marge forward. "Give em a couple. A real taste of human culture for Cesar 4."

"Ranawk 6," Ted corrects, as Marge digs a couple of apple-cinnamon fruit bars out of her purse and holds them out, hand trembling. Several of Ted's tentacle-fingers wrap around her hand to take the crinkled plastic from her, and she barely represses a full-body shiver.

"Those look like apple," Seth tells them, before showing them how to unwrap the bars. The aliens follow Seth's instructions and take bites with one of their four mouths: not the ones that speak, but ones with many sharp, black teeth. They both look repulsed.

"You said to eat these, right?" Robert asks.

"Yeah," Seth says, frowning. "You don't like em?" He turns to Marge. "How long've those been in your purse, baby?"

"Couple of months," Marge says, hand wrapping around her mace in her bag.

"Well, those should still be good," Seth says. "Don't got apples on Ranawk 6, then?"

"Apples? No," Robert says. "What's this... what's this flavor?"

"Apple cinnamon," Marge offers.

"She said apple cinnamon," Seth tells them.

"Cinnamon?"

"We need cinnamon," Ted says, opening a chute in the wall and dumping both fruit bars down the hole. "We use it for our energy."

"You use cinnamon for energy?" Marge asks. Seth relays the question.

"Yes, and ginger," Ted tells them.

"And other spices," Robert says. "You have them here?"

"Must be imported," Ted comments, out of the side of a mouth.

"Your cinnamon, it is like… your gasoline to us," Robert explains. Marge furrows her brow.

"I don't think I have any cinnamon," Marge says. "Just the apple cinnamon fruit bars."

"Oh, shit," Seth says, and both aliens appear shocked.

"*What?*" Robert demands.

"Oshit has been dead for *years,*" Ted tells them.

"Has it?" Seth says. "I'm not up on the trends." He turns back to Marge. "Peggy say anything about that one being out of date?"

"We are *so* sorry," Ted continues. The gleaming room around him reflects off of him like so many tiles on a disco ball when he moves towards Marge; it produces a disorienting glare on the eyes, and Marge involuntarily inches away. "Tell her we mean her no harm, Seth. We just want to help you get home."

"What?" Seth asks. "I thought you needed us."

"They may have the last knowledge of a dead galaxy," Ted says to Robert. "We have the excess energy now from their bar anyways."

"We'll trade them," Robert says, after a moment of thought. Marge's hand loosens around her mace, but Robert turns towards her anyways. Another eye opened high on what Marge supposes is a forehead. "What does she have there?"

Seth motions for Marge to lift her hand. "Whatcha got, Gin?"

Marge slowly lifts her hand, revealing her can of mace. Seth looks disappointed.

"They've been nothing but kind, Gin. Come on," he says. He turns back to the aliens. "I'm so sorry about that. She's just a nervous nellie. Always has been."

"Can we have that?" Ted asks, pointing several hands at the can. Seth frowns.

"Uhh," he says. He turns to Marge. "Can they?"

"Uh-huh," Marge says, holding it out. Ted's fingers leaves slimy trails up her wrist again. She wipes them off on her dress. Ted chucks the can into the chute again, and a few green lights light up around the room, a small chirping emanating from all corners.

"Perfect," Ted says. "Tell her thanks."

"He said thanks, baby," Seth says. Marge nods, staring at one of the flashing green lights.

"You're welcome," Seth tells Ted. "What'd that do?"

"We have enough power to reclaim Tom and take him home for examination," Robert explains. He extends many arms, and Seth extends one of his own, shaking again. "It has been a pleasure, Seth and Marge Bradbury. Thank you for your snacks and phenomenal intellect."

"Oh, thank *you,*" Seth says. "Real pleasure. Glad to help."

"Me, too," Marge offers.

"She said her, too," Seth translates. The aliens, Robert and Ted both, slither over and wrap themselves briefly around them. Marge closes her eyes and holds her breath; Seth tries to hug them back.

"Send our regards to the people of Earth 3," Ted says, as Robert escorts Marge and Seth back to the shining chrome bench. Marge sits as close to Seth as she can manage without climbing into his lap.

"The boys back home won't believe this for a second," Seth tells them. "I can't wait."

"Tell your friends we said hello, too," Marge says. They blink many eyes at her.

"She said to tell your pals hi, from us," Seth says. They nod, Marge assumes.

"Of course," they reply. "We will exchange you for your friend, Tom. Thank you again."

"Anytime, fellas," Seth says, and the two of them begin to blur out of existence once more. Marge feels herself fading, then becoming reinvigorated, and before she knows it, she's back at the table at the church potluck, staring down at the roast beef on her paper plate once more.

"And another thing—" Thomas is saying, as if he hasn't stopped talking since they left. Seth scooches his chair closer to Marge's.

"Have a good one, Tom," Seth says, watching Thomas' bewildered face as he fades out of existence, leaving behind a vacant chair. He glances to Marge. "We should put in a bid for his land when it goes up at auction. Junior's been looking for a place to settle down with that girl of his."

An awful truth dawns on Marge as she considers the implications of such a statement. Abruptly, darkly, a new light is thrown onto Seth's decision to volunteer Thomas so willingly. She looks at him sidelong, and she says, "Seth... did you, um..."

"Yeah, baby?" Seth asks, starting to eat his mac and cheese with Thomas' fork. Marge stares at the goodly man she has been married to for thirty-five years, then at the empty seat beside him. Then, she remembers all the times Thomas has interrupted her while she was talking, taken the last cookie from the dessert tray, and cut her off in traffic, among other things — like refusing to sell his land to their son.

In the end, maybe Seth's decision isn't so wrong after all. We all have to make sacrifices in this world.

"Never mind," she says with a smile. She turns back to her roast beef. "Yeah, we should. Be a nice gift, if we can afford it."

"We'll give it our best shot," Seth says. "New position open at the Grab'n'Go. Junior could help us pay off the land if he wanted."

Marge stares at her roast beef slice again, then took a bite. "Thanks, honey."

"Anytime, baby," Seth says, shoveling mac and cheese in his mouth. "Anytime at all."

PHANTASM

Emily and June have been making their living ghost-hunting for a couple of years, which would be more impressive and brave if June believed in ghosts.

"What've we got today?" June asks, tugging on her wide brown trouser pants. Emily flicks through the notebook she's got in her lap, sitting cross-legged on the bed in June's shirt. June's easily a foot taller than Emily, so her clothes fit like pajamas.

"It's the Glendale Axe Murder House," Emily tells her. She digs a pencil out of the drawer in their bedside table and makes a note in the margin on the page.

"That name alone is gonna cause problems with the house, I won't lie to you," June says, "if for no other reason than it's now the perfect target for neighborhood— hooligans, and the like—"

"Hooligans?" Emily repeats. "What are you, my dad?"

"God, I hope not." June fastens her pants and shakes out her hair. "Have you packed?"

"I will," Emily tells her. She flips through another page of her notes. "In the winter of 1892, six members of the Woodhouse family and two guests in the home were found bludgeoned to death by an axe—"

"Hence the name of the *Axe Murder House,*" June interrupts. Emily glares at her. "Sorry, sorry, go ahead."

"They were found bludgeoned to death by an axe," Emily repeats, "but they never found the murder weapon or the murderer. The family that's living in there right now — the Whaleys, that's Lee and Geraldine and they've got three kids — and they said there's been… uhh, doors slamming, the kids feel like they get pinched or slapped or punched sometimes, there's cold spots in the house—"

"Sounds like a poltergeist, right?" June asks.

"Yeah, they've also found things stacked or thrown around," Emily tells her. She scribbles something else down, then slams the notebook shut and drops it on the bed. "Definitely could be a poltergeist."

"I'll pack for one," June says. They keep a chest full of their ghost-hunting equipment at the foot of the bed, and June digs through it while Emily sprawls backwards on the bed and dangles her head upside-down next to her. "Holy water, Bible, crucifixes, tape recorder."

"Bring that black sweater you've got," Emily tells her. June glances at her. Emily's just absent-mindedly dragging her fingers through her long, dark hair. The tips of her hair brush the floor.

"Why?" June asks. Emily smiles at her.

"Because it's cute," Emily says. "Why else?"

June pushes Emily away with a hand over her face, and Emily just rolls off the bed, laughing as she goes.

The two of them land in a tiny airport in Glendale, Iowa just after five in the morning, so June drives them to their motel while Emily lightly dozes in the passenger seat of their rented Pinto. The Iowa countryside is absurdly flat, and June can see nothing but cornfields and the occasional house or barn dotting the landscape. The sun won't rise for another hour or two, but dawn is starting to bleed into the air, and June watches the sky more than she watches the road.

The motel proves to be about as nice as the other motels they stay in, which is to say it's fine for their purposes. June carries Emily in and drops her on the bed before she jogs back out to get their bags. Iowa is chilly in the mornings in October, so she turns up the heat before she goes back outside. Emily, eyes still shut, gives her a grateful, sleepy half-smile before burying her face in the motel pillow.

Against all odds, the two of them are up, dressed, and ready to go by nine o'clock. Emily is yawning, leaning up against

June's side as they stand on the curb outside the house they're supposed to be cleansing.

"Do you think they're home?" Emily asks, glancing at the house. June hefts her bag up over her shoulder.

"They're supposed to be ready for us at nine," June tells her. She looks at Emily's watch. "It's nine-oh-six."

"Fashionably late," Emily says. June kisses the top of her head, locks the car, and lets Emily lead the way up to the house.

The thing is, they've been ghost-hunting for a while now. They've been together for five years, and June's known since the moment they met that Emily was a little eccentric. The first thing Emily said to her was, "Have you heard about the Black Dahlia murder?", so things kicked off right away. Emily's always been into the murders and crimes and ghosts and all that. June loved her for it, even though she didn't necessarily believe in poltergeists and spirits and demons and all that bullshit. She believed in Emily; that was all that really mattered.

Two years ago, their next-door neighbor, Katherine, came running over, banging on their door at two in the morning. June's the lighter sleeper, so she got up to let Katherine in. Katherine had sobbed through a story about hearing footsteps and knocks in her house when nobody was home. June just shook Emily awake, and Emily listened to the whole thing with her full attention. She'd looked back at June, and June had just put her hand on her shoulder as Emily offered them both up to go over and check out the house.

Emily had suggested that maybe they try to do this for *other* people, once they succeeded in doing it for Katherine. Or, "succeeded," as June often put air quotes around it when she said it. She didn't believe in it. She let Emily do all the actual ghost-hunting and getting rid of the "ghosts," while June was more of the people person, reassuring whoever's house they were in and mostly serving as the business end of things: finding them jobs, arranging everything, then acting as back-up and for someone for Emily to bounce off of while they were actually on the job. She's the showman, the businessman, and the schmoozer; Emily is the genuine one. It's how they act most of the time, anyways, so it transitions well into the business. They've got enough of a good reputation now with this thing that this is what they make their living off of.

They own their own house in a small town in Massachusetts, they travel the country doing what Emily loves to do, and they make enough money to live comfortably. It's really all June can think to ask for.

"So," Emily says, as they stand on the family's porch and wait for someone to answer their knock at the door. "Two kids?"

"Three," June corrects her. "I'll take the adults, you talk with the kids?"

"Sounds good," Emily says. She tosses a grin back at June just as the door opens, and then the screen door is being pushed out.

"You must be the Sharps," a woman says to them. June smiles. Their whole schtick is that they're sisters who hunt ghosts, even though Emily is clearly half-Filipina and June's mother was Nigerian (her father is Romanian). Nobody's called them out on it yet; people who can tell they're together give them knowing looks or smiles, and people who don't want to notice just pretend they don't. June's best guess is they assume they're adopted sisters. Regardless, it's all worked out so far.

"That's us," Emily says, smiling. "I'm Emily, and she's June."

"Sure am," June says, reaching around Emily with her hand out. The woman shakes it. "I'm the one you spoke with on the phone."

"Of course," the woman replies. She's every inch the short, round, blonde Midwesterner that June was expecting. "I'm Geraldine, you can just call me Gerri. Lee and the kids are in the kitchen. Can I get you two anything to eat? Anything for breakfast? Have you eaten?"

"We haven't," June says, at the same time Emily reaches out and takes Gerri's hand between both of hers.

"It's going to be okay, Gerri," Emily tells her. Gerri runs a hand over her face with her other hand. "We're going to help you."

"Okay," Gerri breathes. Her eyes are wet, a little glassy. Emily squeezes her hand. Gerri is about Emily's height, so June has to duck down slightly to meet her eyes.

"We're going to do everything we can," June reassures her. "You're safe with us, I promise. We haven't failed yet. Right?"

"Right," Emily agrees. Gerri brushes a tear off her face and gives a choked little half-laugh.

"Sorry, I'm sorry," she says, and she has the sweetest Midwestern accent. "You probably see all sorts of problems, I'm just overreacting—"

"Gerri, there is no overreacting in situations like this," June tells her. "You're scared. You have every right to be scared. Something's happening in your house." The fact that June believes it's probably the kids playing pranks or one of the parents accidentally guiding the rest of them into some sort of folie à deux situation is beside the point. Gerri's still scared regardless of what's *actually* happening, which is usually what makes the job more realistic, for June. They're here to help, whether it just be a placebo or not.

"We're going to help," Emily says.

"Especially since you're giving us breakfast," June jokes, and it works. Gerri laughs, and the tension and stress of the moment break. Gerri squeezes Emily's hand and lets go, turning to lead them into the house.

"Lee! The Sharps are here!" Gerri calls into the house. A red-haired man who June can only assume is Lee is in the kitchen Gerri brings them to, seated at a small table with two little boys and a baby girl. The girl has smashed fruit all over her face, and the boys are diligently eating eggs on either side of their father.

Lee stands up, dusts himself off, and holds out a hand. "Pleasure to meet you ladies."

"Pleasure's all ours," June says, shaking his hand. Emily shakes it next.

"Now, you know I think this is all horseshit," Lee says, and the boys' heads snap up to look at him.

"Lee," Gerri hisses, admonishing. June almost laughs, except for how embarrassed Gerri looks.

"Well, it is," Lee says. "Ghosts and whatever the heck else you was saying— demons and all that. It's not real. I don't know why I even agreed to all this—"

"Sir, regardless of what's going on, we're here to help," June says. Emily looks a little surprised, so June just keeps going. "Whether or not you believe in spirits, something is going on here in your home. We'll figure out what it is and we'll help you stop it. It may or may not be ghosts, but no matter what, we're here to help. Alright?"

Lee glances back to Gerri. His expression softens a bit just looking at her face, and when he turns back to June, he says, "Yeah, alright."

"Okay, good," June says. The boys are staring up at her. "Hi, there."

"You're so tall," one of the boys breathes. June laughs, "How tall are you?"

"I'm six-foot-five," June says. "But my shoes give me four inches, so I'm six-nine, right now."

"*Wow,*" the other boy says. He scrambles out of his chair, and his brother follows suit, both of them standing in front of June to compare their heights. They look like twins, maybe six years old, and they only come up to her hips. They're delighted by the difference.

"What's your name?" the first boy asks.

"June Sharp," June tells him. "What's yours?"

"Bobby," the boy says. He points to his brother. "That's Will."

"Hi," Will says. Bobby points over his shoulder at the baby.

"That's Suzie," Bobby tells her. June extends a hand to Susan.

"It's a pleasure to meet you, Suzie," June says. The boys both laugh.

"She doesn't know how to shake hands yet!" Will exclaims. "She's only a baby."

"Oh, pardon me," June says. Bobby reaches up to tug on her other hand.

"Do you want some eggs?" Bobby asks. He turns to Gerri. "Can we give June some eggs?"

"We certainly can," Gerri says. She guides June and Emily to two empty chairs opposite Lee at the table and leaves them there while she bustles back over to the stove and starts cracking eggs. June doesn't argue, because all they've had so far today was stale muffins they got at a gas station on the way to the motel.

From the way Bobby and Will won't stop gushing to June about what they've been doing in school and about the things their baby sister does, June mentally switches their plan so she'll take the kids and Emily will talk to Gerri and Lee. She glanced up at Emily and nods her head in Lee's direction, and Emily nods.

"So," Emily says, as she pours herself a bit of orange juice. "What exactly has been going on here?"

"What did Gerri already tell you?" Lee asks.

"Somebody scratched me," Will says, before June can answer. They all look down at him. "While I was sleeping."

"Someone keeps slamming our door," Bobby adds. "And slapping me."

"And me," Will says. "And Suzie."

Suzie doesn't say anything, so Bobby continues, "Sometimes the house gets really cold. Or just one room gets cold."

"There's knocks on the walls," Gerri adds in from the kitchen. "I hear them day and night. Just, somebody banging on the walls in rooms I'm not in, but there's nobody there when I check. The furniture moves around while nobody's home, or while we're in another room."

"Things fly around sometimes," Will says. "Like books."

"Sometimes there's writing on the walls," Bobby tells them. "I can't read it."

"It says disgusting things," Gerri says. "Brutal things. I don't read them to the boys."

"How do you not believe something is happening?" Emily asks Lee. Lee shrugs.

"Boys will be boys," Lee says, with a pointed look down at his sons. Will frowns down at his plate, but Bobby screeches his chair backwards, shoving off from the table so he can stand on his chair and be on eye level with his father.

"I told you it's not us!" Bobby exclaims. Lee stands up.

"You will *not* speak to me that way," Lee shouts back at him. Bobby doesn't back down, which June's pretty impressed by. Gerri seems frozen in place in the kitchen, and Emily looks stunned.

"But it's not us!" Bobby says. "I would never hurt Suzie! You don't believe me—"

"Knock it off *right now,*" Lee tells him, voice loud and angry, but Bobby still doesn't sit back down. Lee raises his hand, and there's a *bang* in an adjacent room. The moment breaks: Suzie starts screaming, Bobby clambers down off his chair and away from his father, and Emily rockets into the other room. Bobby and Will both run after Emily, so June stays, just for a moment, until Gerri follows after them, so the two of them aren't alone together. She already doesn't trust Lee.

Once they're all in the living room, it's clear what's happened: a huge armchair has been flung sideways at the wall. They all stand there for a moment, staring at it, before Emily starts digging through her purse. She pulls out her crucifix and holds it up.

"Whatever spirit is present with us right now, I beg you to leave," Emily says, stern. June takes her purse from her shoulder and pulls the holy water out, sprinkling it in the corners of the room. Bobby and Will follow her as she goes.

"Leave this home!" Emily exclaims. She presses the crucifix to the armchair, and suddenly stumbles backwards, like somebody's shoved her, only there's nobody close enough to touch her. June jumps for her, catches her before she can trip over her own feet.

"What the heck was that?" Lee asks. June helps Emily steady herself before she turns to him.

"That's an angry spirit," June tells him. She doesn't know what it *actually* is, but she's the showman, so she says, "You pissed it off."

"I pissed off the gosh darn *ghost?"* Lee scoffs, turns away. "This is such a load of horseshit."

"Lee, please, not in front of—" Gerri says, but Lee stops her.

"What, in front of the kids? They're the ones playing the stupid pranks," Lee interrupts her. "Or in front of the *sisters?"*

"I don't appreciate your tone," June tells him, injecting as much ice into her voice as she can. Emily glances backwards at her, an obvious warning in her expression.

"Oh, you don't appreciate my *tone,"* Lee replies. "Well, excuse *me* for having a *tone* when you come into my house, telling me I'm pissing off angry spirits that don't actually exist."

"Sir, please calm down," Emily says. She steps neatly in between the two of them, her crucifix still in one hand. "We're here to help."

"We don't need *help*," Lee tells them. "Get the hell out of my home."

"Sir—" Emily starts to say, as Gerri says, "Lee, please—"

"Get the *hell out*," Lee snaps, and then flinches backwards, one hand over his face. One of the boys cries out, and June looks down to see it was Will, who's looking at his arm with confusion.

"Something pinched me," Will says. When June looks back up at Lee, he has scratch marks down his cheek, like nails on his skin. Gerri scoops Will up into her arms, and June can hear Suzie start screaming again in the other room. Gerri takes Will out of the room, running back to her daughter in the kitchen. Bobby backs up until he's behind June's legs.

"How the heck did you do that?" Lee demands. Bobby shakes his head frantically, and June puts her hand on his head, keeping him safely behind her. "You son of a bitch—"

"Lee, *stop,*" Emily orders him, but he shoves past her, knocking her to the ground. June twitches to go to her, but she doesn't want to leave Bobby alone. Emily catches herself with her arms, rolls to stop herself from banging her head on the table, and stands back up without injury. June backs up, Bobby still behind her.

Abruptly, Lee shifts backwards. He looks frustrated, red-faced and enraged, but he can't take another step. June watches, baffled, as he suddenly shudders backwards, then moves like he's being yanked, slamming back into the wall.

"What the hell," June manages, choked. She crouches and scoops Bobby up, holding him on her hip, and he's shocked enough to let her. Emily scrambles over to her and grabs June's hand, then tugs her out of the room, the three of them sprinting for the kitchen.

"Get the kids out of the house," Emily shouts, as soon as Gerri's in her line of vision. June tries to pass Bobby off, but he won't let go of her neck.

"Bobby, it's going to be okay—" June tries to tell him, but he shakes his head, burying his face in her hair. There's a *slam* in the other room.

"We're going to get rid of them, okay?" Emily says. June doesn't know who she means when she says "them," but she says it so firmly that June can't help but believe her. "You're going to be okay. But you *have* to go outside right now, okay?"

"Okay," Gerri says, at the same time the back door slams shut. Will screams, and Suzie starts crying all over again. Gerri tries to put Will down, but he won't go. Emily holds her arms out, and he goes to her. Gerri holds Suzie, and the three women stand there for a moment, unsure of what to do. Then, there's another bang in the next room.

"Daddy's gonna—" Bobby starts saying, but June doesn't have enough of a chance to listen to him before she sees Lee come wheeling around the corner. A long scratch forms on the wall as he goes, but he's not touching the wall. June has absolutely no explanation for what's going on, but her adrenaline's kicked in so much she doesn't care — she just knows she has to do *something,* and Lee is the most immediate threat.

June passes Bobby off to Emily, and heads straight for Lee, landing a solid punch across his cheek and nose that knocks his head to the side. He stumbles backwards, bumping into the kitchen wall, and June backs off, resetting herself in case he comes again. The kitchen cabinets all fly open at once, and food starts pouring off the shelves and onto the floor. Gerri narrowly avoids a box of crackers hitting Suzie as she ducks onto the ground, covering her daughter with her body. Emily backs into the corner, holding both boys tightly against herself.

"Lee, *stop,*" June snaps. Lee shakes off the punch and doesn't listen, moving for June now, seemingly having forgotten about Gerri and the boys completely. "Lee!"

"Fuck you," Lee snarls, and June shoves him back. He lunges at her, wrapping his arms around her and knocking her to the ground underneath him. Gerri screams, but June just kicks at him. He manages to land a hit on her eye before he's suddenly flying backwards, as if he got tugged up to the ceiling by an invisible rope. He hovers by the ceiling fan for a second before he drops down to the linoleum. June scrambles backwards on her hands and feet.

"Holy hell," June breathes. She shoves herself to her feet and backs up until she's in front of Emily, Gerri, and the kids. "Lee, you have to stop. Whatever this thing is, you're angering it, so you have to calm down."

"Gerri," Lee says, ignoring June as he staggers to his feet. "Gerri, don't listen to this bitch. Get over here."

June doesn't have to look backwards to know Gerri isn't moving. They all stand there, stock-still, for a long moment, before Lee takes a step forward, then another, then—

He stops.

He tries to push forward, but it looks like he's pressed against an invisible wall. The scratches on his face are sluggishly oozing blood, and he looks a little worse for wear, but nothing that suggests he'd be unable to walk. He tries to shove forward again, but he just can't seem to. A hazy shape appears in front of him in the next moment, and June truly can't understand what she's seeing anymore.

June blinks, and the shape forms a little more clearly. It seems to be a woman, in a poofy, old-fashioned dress. Probably from the turn of the century, if June had to guess, and then she remembers: the axe murders in this house were in 1892.

"You must stop," the woman says, in a watery, echoing sort of voice. She looks back at June and Emily. "I mean no harm. Please don't banish me from this house. I only want to help."

"Okay," Emily breathes, still behind June. June can't even speak.

"My husband is still here," the woman says. "He torments us. He torments the children, and yours as well. I try my best to keep him away, but he returns every time. Will you help me?"

"Of course," Emily says. June nods dumbly. The woman beckons them forward. "Annie, I'm so sorry for what happened to you."

"It is the past," the woman — apparently named Annie — says.

"Your husband killed you?" Emily asks, as she steps around June and closer to the spirit of Annie Woodhouse. Bobby and Will both let themselves be set on the ground, and they retreat back behind June, to their mother.

"Albert killed me, my sisters, and five of my children," Annie tells her. "My eldest daughter and two eldest sons weren't

189

home — they hid from him, after. They've since found me, and assured me they lived long, happy lives. Albert never found them."

"You've been trying to protect them from Albert," Emily says. Annie nods.

"And Lee," Annie says, turning away from Emily to look at the living, breathing man staring at her. His rage is palpable, but so is his confusion and his complete and utter bewilderment. June can relate. "He reminds me so much of Albert." She glances back, past Emily, past June, to Gerri. "I did not want to see what happened to me happen to you, Geraldine. I was so afraid."

"Thank you," Gerri says, softly. "I'm sorry."

"Never apologize for this," Annie says. She looks back to Emily. "You must help me rid this house of Albert. My children and I are still here, and we try our best to keep Albert and Lee at bay, but we can only do so much."

"We'll do everything we can," Emily promises. She reaches out a hand, but it goes through Annie's wavering, translucent fingers. Emily looks over her shoulder at June. "We promise."

———

It takes a lot of effort, but June manages to twist Lee's arms behind his back and tie his wrists together. She all but drags him into the living room while Emily runs out to the car to get their duffle bag of exorcism supplies. June has no idea what they're going to do, since most of their supplies are for show and they've never actually *seen* a spirit before, but there's really no other option.

Gerri sits on the floor in the corner of the room, all three of her children in her lap, and watches them silently. Emily and June tear the rug off the floor, shove furniture out of the way, and draw any and every exorcism rune and symbol they can think of onto the wood floors underneath with chalk. When they finish, June digs up the salt and lines the room with it while Emily nails crosses and crucifixes to each wall. Lee curses at them the whole time, but they both ignore him. He's still bound, sitting in the middle of the room, wrists and ankles tied with rope from the duffle bag.

"Did you bring sage?" June asks, and Emily nods. June digs the sage out from an inside pocket of the bag and lights both ends. She has no idea if it'll do anything, but she's willing to attempt everything at this point. She's way out of her depth, but Emily just keeps moving, looking terrified but not stopping.

June cleanses the room with burning sage. Emily takes the bundle from her halfway through.

"Anoint the windows and doors," Emily tells her. June goes to do it.

"Are you a priest?" Gerri asks. June shakes her head as she anoints the front window with the sign of the cross. She shuts the curtains after she finishes.

"I was a nun for a week," June says. "Changed my mind." She glances back at Emily, then, for Gerri's benefit, smiles. "Wouldn't you?"

Gerri huffs an almost-laugh, smiling a little. Her terror is still obvious on her face, but at least she trusts them enough to let them help.

Annie watches the whole thing from a doorway, until June kicks a little salt away and lets her in. She sits beside Gerri on the floor and speaks softly to her as June rebuilds the salt perimeter and finishes anointing the room. She can't hear what they're saying, but she figures it's not for her to hear, anyways.

Lee keeps writhing on the floor, but then Emily shuts all the lights off and beckons June to join her in the center of the room. They stand on the center rune — a quickly-drawn pentagram — just the two of them with Lee. Emily hands over their Bible.

"I'll light the candles," Emily says. "Start getting ready for the summoning."

June has summoning spells and exorcism verses memorized. She's hoping that they actually work beyond convincing people that they work from how interesting they sound, because, right now, it's all she has.

Emily lights the candles around the room, then kneels down next to June, putting a hand on the back of Lee's neck and holding him in place.

"Do it," Emily says. June stands firmly in the center of her pentagram, and stares at the second pentagram on the floor beside her. She digs one of their summoning potions out of the duffle bag and spills it over the second pentagram.

"Albert Woodhouse, I summon and bind your spirit," June says, loudly and clearly. "Step forward into our realm and let yourself be known." She takes a deep breath, centers herself, then says, "*Lirach Tasa Vefa Wehlic, Belial. Renich Tasa Uberaca Biasa Icar,*

194

Albert. *Ganic Tasa fubin, Flereous. Jedan Tasa hoet naca, Leviathan. Tasa reme laris,* Albert. Come to us, now."

The candles all blow out at once, casting them into complete darkness. They flicker back to life a heartbeat later, and there's a man standing in the second pentagram. He is unmoving, but he stares at June.

"Scum," he spits. June stares at him.

"Good to meet you, too, Al," June says. "In the Name of Jesus Christ, our God and Lord, strengthened by the intercession of the Immaculate Virgin Mary, Mother of God, of Blessed Michael the Archangel—"

"Stop," Albert orders her. June doesn't stop; she has verses and verses of exorcism rituals, and she recites them each, one by one. Albert reaches for her, but cannot touch her. He screams obscenities at her, but she does not stop speaking. Emily holds Lee to the ground beneath them.

"We drive you from us, whoever you may be, unclean spirits, all satanic powers, all infernal invaders, all wicked legions, assemblies and sects," June says, and Albert shrieks, flickering in and out of sight. "God the Father commands you." June tugs her crucifix necklace off and reaches over, pressing it to Albert's forehead. Albert screams. "God the Son commands you." She looks down at Emily. "Nail him with holy water."

"Got it," Emily says, and she flicks holy water out of a vial at him, and he writhes away from its burning touch.

"God the Holy Ghost commands you," June says, and Albert flickers again, still screaming. June doesn't dare look away from him, but she can hear Suzie crying in the corner still. "O Lord, hear my prayer. And let my cry come unto Thee. May the Lord be with thee. And with thy spirit. Let us pray."

"Amen," Annie murmurs behind them.

"From the snares of the devil," June continues. "Deliver us, O Lord. That Thy Church may serve Thee in peace and liberty—"

"We beseech Thee to hear us," Emily responds.

"That Thou may crush down all enemies of Thy Church," June says.

"We beseech Thee to hear us," Emily repeats.

"Stoop beneath the all-powerful Hand of God; tremble and flee when we invoke the Holy and terrible Name of Jesus, this Name which causes hell to tremble, this Name to which the Virtues, Powers and Dominations of heaven are humbly submissive, this Name which the Cherubim and Seraphim praise unceasingly repeating," June says.

"Holy, Holy, Holy is the Lord, the God of Hosts," Emily adds. June is overwhelmingly glad that she remembers her parts in all of this. It's like a horrible script, and June is nothing if not a rule-breaker, so she goes a little off-book in the next part.

"Begone, Satan, inventor and master of all deceit, enemy of man's salvation," June says, then adds, "Begone, Albert Woodhouse, worse than Satan, for you are a man who has taken the lives of the innocents. For this, you will be forever condemned. I banish you from this home and from this realm, and I banish you to hell. In the name of the Father, the Son, and the Holy Spirit, I cast you out."

Albert screams, flickers again, then is gone. The pentagram is empty, and the curtains all fly open, letting in the morning sunlight. Lee lays gasping on the floor under Emily's hands, and June stumbles backwards, falling to the ground, unable to keep her own legs sturdy under herself.

"Are you okay?" Emily asks. June can't answer, not until she's sure—

She turns back to Annie, looks at her and says, "Is he gone?"

Annie nods, and June fully collapses, burying her face in her arms on the floor and struggling to catch her breath. Emily lays down beside her, stroking her hair.

"You did such a good job," Emily tells her. "Really. You did an amazing job. I'm so proud of you."

"We should call the police," June says. "For Lee."

"Fuck you," Lee spits. Emily nods, gets up, and goes to Gerri.

"Can we call the police?" Emily asks. Gerri just nods, and Annie stands from her place on the ground beside her.

"You will always be safe in this home, Geraldine Whaley," Annie says. "I promise you this. You and your children will always be safe with me and mine."

"Thank you," Gerri breathes. Annie inclines her head to her, then vanishes. Emily looks over her shoulder at June, but

June just shakes her head, because she truly can't process any of this right now.

June, eventually, hauls herself to her feet and goes to find the house phone while Gerri, Emily, and the boys clean up the living room. Lee remains on the floor, still bound, screaming at them all. The boys have tears running down their faces, but they don't look at him.

The police show up quickly after June calls them. She goes outside to meet them, heart still pounding, and tells them the story they all agreed on: that Gerri called them for help with what she assumed was a ghost, but it was really her boys playing tricks. While they were there, Gerri told them how Lee had been treating her and their children, which angered Lee so much he tried to attack them. Emily and June subdued him and called the police, and that's all that happened.

"Thank you," Gerri says, as Lee is being dragged out to one of the police cruisers out front, screaming at them the whole way. Gerri's clutching Suzie close to her chest. Will and Bobby are on either side of her, holding onto her skirts. "I didn't— I don't—"

"It's okay," Emily tells her. Gerri nods, and Emily pulls her into an embrace. "If you need anything, at all, you can just call us, okay? We'll come right back."

"Will you stay the night?" Gerri asks. Emily looks back at June. "Please. Just the night. I don't— Well, I want you to stay for my own sake, but I just hate the image of you two staying in a motel when I have a perfectly nice guest room already made up."

Emily looks at June still, raises an eyebrow and sort of inclines her head. She obviously wants to stay, and June does, too, so June says, "We'd love to. Anything's better than the mattress at that place, even your ghost-infested house."

Gerri laughs; it's a wet, slightly manic sound, but it's a laugh nonetheless. Emily hugs her again, and June just puts her hand on Gerri's shoulder, and doesn't think about the larger implications of everything.

It isn't until that night, as they lay in the bed of Gerri's guest bedroom, both staring up at the darkened ceiling, that June finally says, "Jesus fucking Christ."

"I know," Emily says. June reaches out, and Emily goes, turning onto her stomach, half-laying on top of June. June wraps an arm around her and settles, Emily's weight a solid, grounding presence when she otherwise feels like she might just dissipate into fog and float away.

"Jesus fucking *Christ,*" June repeats. Emily buries her face in June's skin, nose pressed into the hollow at the bottom of her throat.

"I know," Emily says again. "It's going to be okay."

"I can't believe you were right," June says. "Unless this was some kind of— I don't know, shared delusion— Oh, wait, maybe—"

"You can't logic your way out of this one, hotshot," Emily tells her.

"My life is crumbling before my eyes," June says. "Let me have logic to hold my brain together."

"You're like me now," Emily says.

"I don't know about that."

"You're a *believer*," Emily continues. June shakes her head, buries her face in the crown of Emily's head. Her hair still has the familiar scent of her shampoo, and that's even more grounding.

"I don't know what I saw," June says.

"You know *exactly* what you saw," Emily argues.

"Either way," June says, "man is the most dangerous game. I could've told you that one."

"At least we helped," Emily tells her. "We helped Annie *and* Gerri. We got rid of two monsters today."

"That's something," June agrees. They're silent for a long while, laying there in the darkness. Emily's breathing starts evening out, and June rubs her back, just stroking her fingertips lightly up and down the length of her spine as she thinks.

"We saw a fucking ghost," June says, abruptly, into the space between them.

"Two ghosts," Emily says. "Now, please, let me sleep."

"I don't know how you can sleep after today," June tells her, but she goes quiet anyways. Emily's even breathing, her steady pulse, her calming weight — they all drag June towards sleep, even as she struggles to grasp what *happened*.

Some monsters, she eventually thinks, aren't meant to be understood or compromised with or entertained. Some monsters are just meant to be stopped.

STOMPING GROUNDS

This is Fox Hancock's first heist. It's the family business, so he's been waiting for a very, *very* long time for the opportunity, but it's his twenty-first birthday and he's finally been invited along as a birthday gift from his Uncle Isaac. He's never really gotten along with Uncle Isaac, but this might be his last chance to actually participate in a full family heist.

"It might be the last one we ever need," Isaac says, as he lays out blueprints on the coffee table at Fox's birthday party. "It has everything. We will come out of this as very rich men."

"And women," says Isaac's wife, Claire. Isaac glares at her.

"Claire, shut your mouth," Isaac tells her. "You're lucky I'm even letting you come."

Fox looks down at the table. His mother always told him not to get involved with other people's affairs, but it's hard to watch Aunt Claire's face when things like this happen.

"We're going to a museum," Isaac tells the people gathered. It is the two of them, Aunt Claire, Uncle Jacob, Uncle Terry, Uncle Eric, and Aunt Alice. His cousins have come, too: Evan, Jonny, Kenneth, Darren, Cynthia, Maurice, Camilla, and Nathan. Grandpa Nick and Grandma Faith sit on the sofa. Fox's own mother and father, Gabrielle and Marvin, sit on either side of Fox. None of these names are important to remember. It is only important that you remember the sheer scope of a Hancock family heist.

"A museum," Fox whispers. "Just like the movies."

"Yeah, just like the movies," Marvin echoes. "Which makes it a dumbass idea. Why do you always go for museums, Isaac? It's stupid as shit."

"Because they'll never expect it there," Isaac tells him. "Now, shut up and listen. We're not going for the money in the vault."

"What?" Claire asks. Isaac slaps her across the face, and she backs off, goes and sits by herself next to Grandma Faith.

"They have a display right now," Isaac says. "It's a little showroom. It's a traveling thing, part of some show in the museum right now, but it's about these crown jewels from some stupid country in Europe or something." Isaac points at a little square on the blueprints. "That's what we're taking."

"How are we supposed to sell those?" Marvin asks. "What are we supposed to do with some goddamn jewels? Do we *look* like jewel thieves?"

"I already got a guy interested," Isaac tells him.

"You do not," Marvin says, and Isaac digs a card out of his blazer pocket and waves it in Marvin's face. Fox hates everyone in the room with a horrible, *blistering* rage.

207

"I do so," Isaac snaps back. He shoves the business card back into his pocket and turns back to the blueprints. He lays out their plan. Each cousin is meant to stand in a certain spot, disguised as security guards. His aunts already have beautiful dresses picked out; they are distractions. His uncles are the muscle. His parents are the bait. Uncle Isaac is the trap.

He, Fox, in the one who has to retrieve the jewels.

"You've never done this before, but you're also the smallest and the most flexible, and we're gonna expect some real fancy security in there," Isaac tells Fox. "It's your inaugural run. We're proud of you."

"Thanks," Fox says, staring down at the blueprints. "Do I get a gun?"

"Hell no," Isaac says, rolling up the papers. He shoves them all into his backpack and stands. Everyone else follows suit. Fox stands, if only not to feel strange for being the only one sitting down. He misses his brother. Sam used to be the only one who made him feel even a little comfortable at these things.

"Meet back here tomorrow," Grandpa Nick says. He stands, too, leaning on a cane and on Grandma Faith's shoulder. "It's a good plan, son."

"Damn straight," Isaac replies. Everybody leaves Fox's house. Gabrielle brings him one of the last cupcakes left, and his parents go to bed. Fox stares at the cupcake for a long, long time before he just eats the thing and goes up to his room.

He hasn't been allowed to move out yet, but that means he knows this house like the back of his hand. He's lived in it for twenty-one years. He knows which floorboards are loose in his bedroom because he is the one who loosened them. He removes the floorboard near the head of his bed, partially underneath the side table on his right side, and tugs the pistol out of the space. It's loaded. It's prepared. He's been practicing shooting for years now, in secret, waiting for this day. It's going to be perfect.

The next day drags. Fox slept with his gun under his pillow, so he has a crick in his neck. He's allowed to take the day off from his classes at his community college; he tells them it's a family emergency. They believe him. He sounds close to tears on the phone. Marvin pats him on the back.

Fox spends most of the morning drifting through the house, drilling himself on the plan Isaac told him the night before. Gabrielle and Marvin are proud of him for his dedication to the heist. Fox looks into Sam's empty bedroom more than once and just stands, staring, in the doorway. His brother's bed is stripped of sheets. His closet is vacant. It's the home of a ghost.

Fox keeps pacing.

As soon as the afternoon hits, the front door opens. Uncle Isaac comes in without knocking, pocketing the key he had made for Fox's house. He didn't ask Gabrielle or Marvin or Sam or Fox if he could have a key. He just had one made. Uncle Isaac is like that.

"Get in the living room, fuckers!" Isaac calls. Fox jogs down the stairs and his whole family is already there, all dressed, all made up, all ready to go. "Let's go, dipshit. You're taking your bike, so you need a head start."

Fox knows there's space in Isaac's car for him, and in Marvin's, and with his grandparents, and probably everywhere else, but he prefers travelling alone. He especially prefers it tonight; he can rely on his bike.

He roars to the museum on his motorcycle, helmet firmly in place. He beats everyone else there, and waits in the parking lot for everybody to show up. They've done this before; they've done this loads of times before, over dozens and dozens of years. This is nothing new. Fox splits off from them right away. He's been going over the plan all day. He knows what he's supposed to do.

When Fox is inside, it's only two minutes before he hears a gunshot. He's startled. He checks the pistol in his jacket, because he's momentarily positive that it must have been his gun; who else could it have been?

People are running, screaming. Fox hides in the bathroom. He can see other feet in other stalls, so in the stall he hides in, he puts his feet up on the toilet seat, so nobody can see him. He hears another gunshot, deep inside the museum. He feels completely blank, completely empty, without emotion. He's only distantly surprised that something's gone wrong in the heist, but only because he knew the plan so well.

The door to the bathroom slams open, and Fox recognizes the voice that enters: it's Uncle Isaac. He sounds panicked, and so Fox sticks his head out of the stall.

"What happened?" Fox asks. Uncle Isaac runs into the stall and bolts it shut behind them.

"Grandma Faith killed your Uncle Terry," Isaac tells him. "This whole thing's gone to shit. Nobody's following my goddamn plan. I don't know why she had to choose *this* plan to go haywire on—"

"Whoa, whoa," Fox says. "Why'd she kill him?"

"Hell if I know," Isaac tells him. "I just know I'm not getting out of here without those jewels." He looks to Fox. "You still in?"

Fox never really liked his Uncle Terry. He doesn't like any of them. He's just mad his Grandma Faith got to do something about it before he did.

"Yeah, I'm still in," Fox says. Isaac claps him on the shoulder.

"Good boy," Isaac tells him. "Let's go."

Isaac opens the stall and leads Fox out, out into the museum, back through the lobby and into the galleries. Distantly, there's more gunfire, and the two of them hide in a tiny alcove while people run by. One of those people is Fox's cousin, Cynthia, and she skids to a stop.

"Half the family's fucking dead," Cynthia says. "They're all shooting each other. What the fuck is going on?"

Isaac pulls out his own gun from his pocket and shoots her in the forehead. He turns to Fox, leveling the gun at him, and motions towards the showroom with the crown jewels in it. "You're just gonna keep coming with me."

"Did you kill Uncle Terry?" Fox asks, calm. He didn't care for Cynthia, either. This whole thing is a goddamn mess, but he's not that broken up about it. Now he's just more concerned about why everyone is killing each other *now,* now that Fox had finally resolved *himself* to handle this problem.

"No, that was your Grandma Faith," Isaac tells him. He peeks around the next corner and, finding the gallery empty, leads Fox through it. "I was planning on it, though."

"Are you gonna kill me?" Fox asks. Isaac shrugs.

"Not if you help me out," Isaac tells him. Fox nods and keeps going with him, follows him through the galleries. They hear the distant sound of continuing gunfire. The galleries are completely empty, now, and by the time they get to the showroom, alarms are blaring and red and white lights are flashing everywhere. Gabrielle is already in the showroom with the jewels.

"Everyone else is dead," Gabrielle says. She motions towards the jewels. "Let's take these and just go, just get out of here."

"Everyone else is dead, Mom?" Fox echoes. Gabrielle nods and points at the jewels.

"That's what I said, so get the goddamn jewels," Gabrielle orders him. Fox goes, sprinting at the jewels and snatching them all up. He hears another gunshot, and he looks back to see his mother slump to the ground. He glances to Isaac, who's pointing the gun at him.

"I'm not gonna do anything," Fox tells him. Isaac glares.

"You better not," Isaac says. "Grab 'em all and let's go."

Fox stuffs the jewels into his pockets, pulling out the gun he's stashed in there as he does so. Once he has the last jewel in the pocket of his pants, he turns and shoots Isaac in the chest. Isaac hits the ground, on his knees, and groans.

"What the fuck?" Isaac grunts. He looks up at Fox and aims his gun, but Fox jumps down and kicks the pistol out of his hand.

"I just wish I could've gotten you all myself," Fox says. "You dumb fuckers. You all tried to turn on yourselves at the same time."

"Fuck you—" Isaac starts to say, and Fox shoots him in the head. He takes the business card out of Isaac's blazer before he bleeds all over it. Then, Fox wipes off the gun and leaves it there, sprinting for the exit. He sobs as he goes; he still looks like a teenage boy when he cries, so security lets him right through.

His helmet is still dangling from his bike. He jogs right past the cops and to the motorcycle, tugging the helmet on, zipping up his jacket, making sure everything is just right. He leaves the museum behind, and feels nothing for the bodies in it. They may as well be strangers for how little he cares about what they've done to each other.

Fox drives three towns over to an all-night diner with a phone booth outside. He uses one of his last coins to call the number on the back of the business card he stole off of Isaac, and arranges for the buyer to come to the diner as soon as possible.

Fox sits on the ground beside his motorcycle in the parking lot. He wonders what Sam would have done, had he been involved tonight. Would he have helped? Would he have understood?

"Sam would have died," Fox says, out loud. Sam was the weaker of the two of them. Fox misses him, sure, but he was the weak link. Grandma Faith always said so, and she was his grandmother. She had to be right.

"What the hell did you say?" somebody asks. It's his buyer. Fox digs all the jewels out of his pockets and hands them over, and receives two duffle bags in exchange. He counts it all in front of the buyer; he's not shortchanged.

"Keep my number," the buyer tells him. The card says his name is Champagne. Fox doubts that but, then again, his name is Fox. "You're one of the Hancocks, right?"

"That's right," Fox says, putting his helmet on and snapping the visor down into place. "I'm the last one left."

"Then I definitely want you to keep my number," Champagne tells him. Fox nods to him as he slings the duffle bags across his chest.

"I'll call you again," Fox says, and peels out of the parking lot, blood spattered on his hands, with no intention of ever looking back.

ISAIAH 14:12

Dana Chambers is probably the most famous actress in the world. She's gorgeous and wealthy and she's a phenomenal actress, truly sensational. Every movie she's in is a hit. If she makes an indie movie, it becomes a blockbuster, if she's in a big-budget movie, it's Oscar-worthy. Everything she touches turns to gold. Everybody loves her. She has a lovely reputation, and she's known for being unbelievably kind. She's everything anyone could ever want to be in this world.

She's also sitting in a coffee shop in Boston like she can just *do* that. Like it's normal for the biggest star in the world to just sit in some podunk coffee place in Boston on a Tuesday and do the crossword puzzle in the back of her newspaper. Ridley can't stop staring at her. Ridley's had a crush on her since she first started on television back when they were both teenagers. It feels surreal to be actually looking at her right now.

People in the place are *obviously* staring at her, but she's totally ignoring them. She seems warm, and welcoming. She's wearing a brown pantsuit. Her blonde hair is honey-perfect. No flyaways. Ridley has to suppress a sigh just watching her.

Eventually, Ridley tugs their headphones out and resolves to walk up and just talk to Dana. They'd never forgive themselves if they passed up the opportunity. They don't even want to ask for a signature or a photograph or anything, not that they wouldn't take one if the opportunity came up organically. They just want to *talk* to her. That's it. That's all.

Ridley squares their shoulders, takes a deep breath— and then the barista calls their name. They turn to take their coffee, face already burning as the barista hands their drink over. They feel like everyone's watching them, like they all knew what Ridley was about to do. When they turn back around, though, nobody is. They're all still normal. Ridley sighs, then straightens up, because Dana's missing. She's not sitting where she just had been. Ridley looks left, frantic, then right, looking for the door, worried they missed their chance in that split second. They take a step without looking and immediately slam into somebody, knocking the person's coffee out of their hand and spilling their own all over them both.

"Oh, God, I'm sorry," Ridley exclaims, trying to brush hot coffee off with their hands. They look up and feel all the blood drain out of their face. It's Dana. "Christ. I'm *so* sorry, I just— I know you."

Dana laughs. Of all things, she *laughs*. "Yeah, probably. It's okay, dude, don't worry about it. At all, for real.." She steps away for a moment and returns with napkins, and the two of them get on their hands and knees to mop up their two cups of coffee. Ridley feels like this is a total fantasy, like it's a dream, like they're not really cleaning up spilled coffee with a famous movie star right now, because how could they *possibly* be doing that? It's something you read in romance novels, not something that happens in real life.

"Are you hurt?" Ridley asks. Dana laughs. "No, really. That was *hot* coffee. I don't want you to burn yourself."

"No, I'm not hurt," Dana tells them. "The dangerous coffee will have to try and assassinate me a different day, because today, I *live.*"

"I'd like to see them try," Ridley says, smiling. The two of them stand and throw all the napkins in the trash. "Let me get you another coffee."

"Oh, no, you don't need to do that, buddy," Dana says. Ridley waves her off. "Really—"

"*You* really," Ridley tells her, and Dana smiles. "I dropped your coffee, I'm getting you a new one. I don't care how rich and fancy you are."

"If you insist," Dana says. Ridley beckons her over to the barista and repeats their order before motioning to Dana, and Dana recites her order back to the barista, as well.

While Dana speaks to the barista, Ridley takes a second to look her over. She's not that tall; she's about a foot shorter than Ridley, anyways. She's got a burgundy turtleneck sweater on underneath a brown blazer, tucked into high-waisted brown pants. She has her hair pinned casually, falling loose down her back. She looks beautiful. She turns to look at Ridley.

"You're too kind," Dana says. "Really. It's too much. I shouldn't've even—"

"I'm the one who spilled coffee all over you," Ridley says. "I mean, at least your pants were coffee-colored already. Maybe nobody'll notice."

Dana smiles. "Yeah, well, at least there's that."

There's silence for a moment, but Ridley always gets uncomfortable easily in silence. "So. What brings you to Boston?"

"Filming," Dana tells them. "I'm working on a new project. It's a whole thing. They made me chop some hair for it."

"Oh, do tell," Ridley says. The barista brings their coffee to the counter, and Ridley takes them both, leading Dana to a table for two people. "Unless you're not allowed to talk about it. I don't really know how these things work."

As Dana turns her head to shake her hair over her shoulder, it looks like her eyes flash, just a moment, entirely black. It's a fleeting thing, and it's gone when Ridley looks again, but they could've sworn they saw it. It could've been a trick of the light. Ridley doesn't think it was, and the chance that it was real excites them.

"I can talk about it," Dana tells them. She puts her elbows on the table and leans forward, smiling. She's got sharp canine teeth. "I can talk *all* about it, but, to be honest, I'd much rather hear all about *you,* though."

Ridley frowns a little, taking a sip of their coffee. "Why? *You're* the interesting one."

"You'd think," Dana says. She leans back and picks up her own coffee. "Well, you have me at a disadvantage, because I still don't know your name."

"Oh," Ridley says. They cup the coffee between their hands; it's warm and makes their hands sweat a little. "It's Ridley."

"That's pretty cool," Dana says. "Cool name, I mean. Very cool."

"Thanks," Ridley tells her. "I grew it myself."

Dana laughs, and a few people in the shop turn to look at her. A lot of eyes linger. Someone picks up their phone and snaps a picture. Ridley can't help but watch them all. She wonders if Dana even shows up on camera; Ridley's had a little bit of trouble with that themselves. It's all a bit overwhelming.

"Do they bother you?" Ridley asks. "Like, do we bother you?"

"One, you're definitely not like them," Dana answers. Ridley feels their face grow hot. "Two, no, it doesn't. If it bothered me, I wouldn't've gotten into it in the first place. I love it, to be honest."

Ridley half-smiles, shrugs. "I wouldn't love it, personally. If I were me. I'm better at focusing on one person at a time."

"They're all focusing on one person," Dana says. "Me."

Ridley laughs. "I guess that's true." They glance back at up at her. "But I'm definitely not like them."

"Oh, not at all." Dana smiles again, then glances down at her watch. She frowns slightly, glancing back up at Ridley. "Are you doing anything tonight? Like, plans-wise? Hanging out-wise?"

"Tonight? No," Ridley lies. They were planning on watching a movie with their roommate, but, God, if *Dana Chambers* asks you if you're busy, you say *no*.

"Perfect," Dana says. "I'm sorry I'm being so rude, they have me on a tight schedule. We can talk more about the movie tonight, if you really want. I'd like to talk all about Ridley, though." Dana pulls out her wallet and removes a business card. "Do you have a pen?"

Ridley digs through their bag and pulls out a pen, handing it over. Dana leans over the table to scribble on the back of the business card before she gives it and the pen to Ridley.

"Send me a text," Dana says. "Tell me when and where to meet you and I'll be there. I'm sure you know all the best spots in town."

Ridley stares down at the card, then up at Dana. "Sure. When are you free?"

"Whenever you need me to be," Dana tells them. Ridley grins. "I'm really sorry I do have to run so quickly. But, I'll see you tonight?"

"Yeah, you sure will," Ridley says. Dana smiles back to them, picks up her coffee, and turns to leave. Her edges blur a little bit as she does, and her eyes flash again. Ridley is delighted, because they know *exactly* what that means, so they know *exactly* what they're going to do tonight. They stuff everything back into their bag and stand, flipping the business card over to read the back.

ridley — evocatio — the city is ours, the card reads. There's a phone number scribbled underneath. Ridley turns to look at Dana's back as she leaves the coffee shop. She's already out the door, and Ridley watches her through the huge windows as she strides down the street. She knows more than Ridley thought she did, and that's just *phenomenal,* because it means Ridley can do exactly what they want to do tonight.

Ridley sticks the business card in their shirt pocket, slings their bag across their chest, and grabs their coffee before heading out the door to work. They're going to be a little late, but it's worth it to meet a kindred spirit.

———————

"You are *not,*" Laurie says from the other room. Ridley laughs, tugging a sweater over their head. "You absolutely just are *not.*"

"I am," Ridley calls back. They button the top button on the button-down shirt underneath their sweater before sliding on leather gloves. They then fasten two chained collar pins across the collar spread. When they come out of their room, Laurie laughs.

"You went with the crosses," Laurie comments, pointing at their collar. "Of course you did. You wanna tempt fate?"

"Aren't we already?" Ridley replies. They slide their boots on and kneel to tie them up. Laure just lounges on the sofa, head dangling upside-down off the arm, hair brushing the floor.

"How sure are you, anyways?" Laurie asks. "Because you could be wrong and then you're gonna just give Dana Chambers some really weird goddamn night she talks about in interviews or something."

"I'm pretty sure," Ridley says. They finish with their boots and stand, spreading their arms. "How do I look?"

"Mephistophelean," Laurie tells them. Ridley snorts.

"Try an English word, you menace," Ridley says. Laurie hauls herself off of the sofa and climbs onto the sofa to sit cross-legged.

"Absolutely fiendish," Laurie offers instead. Ridley grins, bowing slightly. "Get over here, let me do your hair for you."

Ridley sits on the floor in front of Laurie and waits patiently while she combs their hair back and ties it up into a neat bun. Ridley leans back, and Laurie kisses them on the forehead. Their tiny apartment is a dingy mess, but they both have to do their best not to draw too much attention to themselves, and this helps them blend in with the rest of the city. Besides, Ridley really doesn't mind it. It reminds them of home.

"You ready to go on a goddamn date with Dana Chambers?" Laurie asks, eventually. Ridley nods, grinning, and Laurie lets them up. She smacks them on the ass once they're standing. "Go get 'em, tiger."

"Yes, ma'am," Ridley says. They grab their jacket, slide it on, and do a slow turn.

"Stop fishing for compliments and *go,*" Laurie tells them, flinging a pillow off the sofa at them. They slide out of the way and out the front door of the apartment. The stairs down to the bottom floor are dimly lit by a bare bulb, and Ridley jogs down them without a lick of fear in their chest. They whistle as they stroll out the front door, hands in the pockets of their trousers, a light rain misting their face as they head down the street.

Ridley had texted Dana late that afternoon about where to meet, and as they walk, they get slightly less confident about their plan. Laurie's words sit heavily in the back of their mind, but only enough to bring a slight concern that they *might* be wrong. In the end, though, even if they *are* wrong, it'll only be for a short while and Dana can just write it off as a strange night.

Dana Chambers. *The* Dana Chambers. It seems too good to be true, like some sort of dream, and yet.

And yet, here we are.

Ridley comes to a stop outside the church and waits, lingering at the end of the path, glancing down the street. Nobody familiar yet, but the night is young. Ridley leans against a light post and pulls out their phone, but there's no messages. Instead, they just scroll through old emails, barely paying attention, until they hear the click of heels on pavement. It's the only sound besides the buzzing of the light above their head and the distant rush of cars on a faraway road. It's too late for any cars to consider coming down past the church and graveyard.

"Interesting place for a first date, isn't it?" Dana asks, once she's close enough to be heard. Ridley pockets their phone and pushes away from the light post.

"I thought you might like it," they tell her. "Care to join me inside?"

Dana looks them over, then glances at the church. Her head tilts up, and back, and up again, until she's looking at the highest point of the steeple. She smiles a little.

"Yeah, sure, I'd love to," Dana says. She's got a big fur coat on, high heels, impeccable makeup, wavy hair. She looks just how old-timey movie stars are supposed to look. Ridley wonders if that's when she got the idea from. Maybe she's been stuck for seventy years.

Dana leads the way, with the confident step of someone who's pretty sure this won't go badly, while Ridley follows behind, watching her. Dana pushes open the church door and steps inside, and nothing happens.

"That's nice," Dana says, apropos of nothing. She heads inside, into the darkness that Ridley cannot see beyond, and so they follow. The heavy door swings shut behind them with a terrifically final bang, and they are left in blackness and shadow.

"Where are the candles?" Dana's voice asks. Ridley digs in their pocket for a lighter. They raise it up, snap it on, and a small flame illuminates them both. Dana is closer than Ridley had thought she was.

"Over there," Ridley says, and passes off the lighter. Dana takes it to light two small candles, then each candle in the holders at the end of each pew. Soon, the whole church is flickering with that ceaselessly-moving light. The candle flames glow just enough to fill the space, and the two of them look up at the sanctuary. There's a massive crucifix behind the altar, Jesus hanging from the cross, dripping blood. The ornate paintings and architectural detailings surrounding him and the sanctuary are brilliantly gold.

"What made you want to come here?" Dana asks. "Besides the ambience."

"A hunch," Ridley says. They brush past Dana, heading towards the sanctuary. They stop just short of stepping up, then they sit down, cross-legged, on the plush red carpet underneath their feet. Dana comes behind them and lays a hand on their black hair.

"How did you know?" Dana asks. Ridley shrugs.

"Your eyes," Ridley says. "Your teeth. Something about you. I've always felt drawn to you." They turn their head up; Dana's hand slides until it rests on their forehead. "What do you eat?"

"Fame," Dana says. "Attention. People like you— Or, well, people like I thought you were, I suppose— give me so much of it. I've never wanted for it. It's an extension of greed."

"I'll still give you attention." Ridley pushes their head further into Dana's palm. She scratches at their scalp.

"Which sin did you choose?" Dana asks. Ridley smiles.

"Lust," they say. Dana doesn't look down at them, eyes still fixed on Jesus' face, but she does smile.

"That doesn't surprise me," Dana says. "You're very charismatic. Eye-catching. Something about your face... I'm not sure. You're not handsome, but you're just striking. Remarkable. Can't look away from it."

"That was the goal," Ridley tells her. They reach up, wrap their long fingers around her thin wrist, and tug. Dana sits down on the carpet beside them. "Which one are you?"

"Mammon was my parent," Dana says. "You can't expect me to just give you my name, do you?"

"I can try," Ridley says. "Asmodeus was my parent."

"Again, unsurprising," Dana replies.

"How long have you been in Dana Chambers?" Ridley asks. Dana leans over, puts her head on Ridley's shoulder. Ridley keeps looking straight ahead, at the way the candlelight flickers off the golden, shimmering walls and the portraits within their gilded frames.

"Since she was twelve," Dana says. "She was dying, but I could already tell she was going to be talented and beautiful. She was so *funny,* my God, everybody loved her. It was easy to take her over. She's not in here anymore, this is all mine for now."

"That's nice," Ridley replies.

"And who were you?" Dana asks. "You're not exactly a chatterbox, I don't know what your plan was here."

"No plan," Ridley tells them, honestly. "Just happy to meet a kindred spirit."

"Mm," Dana says. "You didn't answer my question."

Ridley reaches over, takes Dana's hand in theirs. They stroke the back of it with their thumb, tracing the fine bones. "Ridley is still in here, somewhere. They stopped trying a while back, though. I've had this body for about seven years."

"Good body to have," Dana comments. "So tall."

"Six-foot-two," Ridley says. "It's about average."

"I love it," Dana tells them. They sit in silence for a little while, just the two of them wreathed in flames. Then, Dana turns her head and kisses Ridley on the cheek. Ridley turns their head, too, and looks down at Dana. When they look down at her hands, she's leaning into the carpet, pressing the pattern of the rug into her palms.

"Is that comfortable?" Ridley asks. Dana snorts.

"Who gives a fuck?" she asks back, and Ridley kisses her on the mouth. It's her sustenance, after all. Nectar of the gods, or whatever the opposite of gods might be. Dana's hands come up, and she hisses, pulling back abruptly, clutching her hands to her chest.

"What the hell was that?" Dana demands, looking down at Ridley's chest. She exhales, shoulders relaxing. "Jesus fucking— Are those crosses?"

"I thought it might be funny," Ridley comments. Dana strokes a loose lock of hair back from Ridley's face, tucking it behind their ear.

"You're not funny," Dana says, and Ridley almost laughs before they're kissing again. God's forgotten children, on the carpet of an empty church, with Jesus' dead eyes staring down at them. It's almost poetic.

"I miss people like me," Ridley whispers. Dana smiles against their mouth.

"People like us aren't people," Dana murmurs back. Her eyes are fully black when she opens them again. "I fell thousands of years ago."

"Eve is my cousin," Ridley jokes, and Dana laughs, nuzzling at Ridley's throat.

"Give me what I want and I'll give you what you want," Dana says, *begs, pleads,* and Ridley does, pins her to the floor of the church and gives her every reason to thank God that He cast her out of heaven when he did. The candlelights flicker over them, filling the church with heat and sin and chaos and death.

The tabloid newspapers and celebrity magazines go wild. Dana Chambers is finally seeing someone, after so many years single, after so many flings and reported one-night stands and countless insistences that she was just the solitary type.

Now, Dana Chambers is on the cover of some gossip rag, hand-in-hand with some lanky dark-haired figure, sunglasses covering up half their face as they smile at the greatest star the world's ever seen. Dana Chambers smiles right back, like they're the sun, the moon, the stars. She would know, because she remembers their creation.

Ravens sit on their roof. Crows sit in the garden. Deer die on their front lawn, and cats flock to the backyard, where breastmilk manifests in puddles like rain. Sage burns in the neighbors' homes; they're too smart for their own good. Laurie moves in across the street and burns incense from her windows.

Movie contracts come. Dana Chambers never seems to grow older. Ridley Walsch never seems to grow younger. They are both still, frozen in time. Candles blaze at night. The church down the street has its locks broken countless times. At night, Dana Chambers whispers, "Morning star."

HYDE AND SEEK

Timothy Tidmarsh has been driving for quite some time now. He drank about two glasses of red wine before he started driving, which he knows is a bad idea, but there's nobody else on the desert roads this late at night, so he's not too worried about crashing into anybody else.

At this point, though, it is about two in the morning, so he's starting to worry about crashing, *period*. The only thing to really crash into is the guardrail, but it's starting to seem like more and more of a threat every time his eyes close of their own accord and he drifts a little, sliding off his half of the road.

The fourth time this happens, Timothy's head snaps up, he swerves back into place, and he says, loudly and forcefully, to himself, "God*damnit!*"

There's nobody to hear him, but just hearing a voice reminds Timothy that he has been driving alone for far too long.

He looks at the sides of the roads, but finds no sign nor any rest step. He was hoping he might be able to just sleep in his car, but all he sees for miles and miles is just sand. In the far, far distance, there's a huge black blob that might, in the daylight, be one of those gigantic orange mountains he saw the day before, but at night, it's just a shadowy shape.

Just as Timothy is contemplating just pulling off into the sand between guardrails and napping there, he sees a new shape. This one has lights on inside of it, and he recognizes it as a mansion of some sort. Here, in the middle of nowhere, there is a grand manor, reminiscent of some old New England monstrosity, strangely placed here on the Western frontier. He doesn't really care who designed it to look like it does or why they did it; he just hopes that there's a parking lot he can sleep in, or *something*.

As it turns out, the place is perfect, because it's not somebody's house; it's an actual hotel. There is a tiny, sandy dirt parking lot, and he pulls in, grateful to finally stand up out of his car and stretch. He's not a small man, and his six-foot-five body is not happy when it's folded up inside his rental car for hours and hours of time. He digs his duffle bag out of the back out of the car and stares up at the hotel.

"Goddamn haunted house," Timothy says, to himself. The parking lot is full of cars, which seems strange for a random hotel in the middle of the woods, but he's exhausted and doesn't give a damn if there's a wedding in the place tonight or something. He locks his rental car and drags himself up the stone steps to the front door of the place. The door is locked, so he rings the doorbell off to the side of what is, apparently, the strangest hotel in existence.

The doorbell rings inside like a church bell clanging high in a tower, and he waits for somebody to answer. It doesn't take long for the door to open, a small man standing in the small opening, looking up at Timothy.

"Can I help you?" the man asks. Timothy stares down at him. It's not that he's odd-looking; it's that he feels like he's two people at once: a man who wants to welcome Timothy in, and a man who wants nothing more than for Timothy to march right back down the stairs and drive away.

"I've been driving a while and was hoping you might have some vacancy," Timothy tells him. His exhaustion wins out over his bewilderment at the man's bizarre expression. He hears church bells again, but he didn't ring the doorbell. The man motions him in, taking a candle off a low table just inside the door.

"We do have a vacancy," the man tells him. "Right this way."

The front door is too heavy to stay open once Timothy lets it go, and it slams shut behind him. The sound echoes with the bells throughout the mansion, but Timothy can't see most of the interior; it's too dark to observe all that much. He can hear music and voices down a couple of hallways that he and the man pass. The man does not stop. He leads Timothy down a far corridor and stops at a seemingly random door.

"This will be you," the man says. He fishes a key out of his pocket and unlocks the door. Timothy can't even see down the rest of the hall as the man hands the key over and motions Timothy inside. "You have a phone inside. If you need anything, call for me. My name is Henry."

"Wonderful," Timothy says, stepping into the room. "Thank you, Henry. What's the—"

"Have a nice night," Henry interrupts him, pulling the door shut. Timothy is plunged into darkness. He fumbles along the wall until he finds a chain and yanks it, and the room is abruptly flooded with light. Timothy blinks, squinting.

The room is ordinary. There's a single bed with a simple wrought iron bed frame, a small wooden dresser, and a desk with a telephone on top. The desk chair is a wooden dining chair from another time, another set that does not match the dresser. Timothy drops his duffle bag on top of the dresser and turns to find a door for the bathroom.

There are no doors, and no windows.

Timothy sighs. He digs his toothbrush out of his bag and heads for the door again, only to find it locked. He stares at the knob for a long, long moment before sighing again and retrieving the key from his pocket. He really doesn't have time for any nonsense or strange goings-on in this place. He just wants to get some shut-eye, pay for the room, and leave the next morning. That's it. That's *all he needs.*

Timothy unlocks the door and steps into the dark corridor again, toothbrush and key in hand. He feels along the wall, hoping to find another door. By the time he gets to one, he doesn't even bother to knock or check anything about the door; it's too impossibly dark to know what the door even looks like. He just opens the door and finds himself staring into a moonlit courtyard.

"You've got to be kidding me," he says, staring at a group of men all dancing to the beat of a jazz band. Every man is wearing red velvet robes and huge colorful hats. Timothy just stares into the courtyard. The men keep dancing, even as Timothy stands in the doorway.

"Sherry?" a man asks at Timothy's elbow. Timothy jumps slightly, glancing at him. He's apparently some sort of butler or a servant, wearing a normal hotel uniform. He holds up a small silver serving tray with several sherry glasses balanced on it. Timothy takes one of the glasses.

"Isn't sherry an apéritif?" Timothy asks. The man looks over the rim of his very small spectacles at Timothy.

"It is, sir," the man says. "They're only just getting ready."

"Goody," Timothy replies, dry. He sips at his sherry. The man walks away. The sherry tastes strange, more viscous than he remembers. He sips at it anyways and shuts the door behind himself, watching the men dance together to the strange jazz beat. He glances around the place. "What year is it?"

"Sixty-nine," a voice answers, this time at his left elbow. He glances down at another strange man.

"Nineteen?" Timothy asks. The man laughs.

"Welcome," the man says. "Do you want ice for your sherry?"

"Nah, it's great like this," Timothy lies. He sips at the glass again. The butler returns and hands the tall man at Timothy's left his own glass of sherry. The man accepts with a slight bow that almost knocks his grand plumage off of his head.

"To the night," the man says. He takes a swig of the sherry, then coughs, turning to Timothy. "How horribly rude of me, I didn't introduce myself. My name is Matthew MacDonald."

"My name is Tim—"

"Wonderful," Matthew MacDonald cuts him off. "Absolutely marvelous. Boys!"

All the men stop dancing and turn to look at Matthew MacDonald. The band stops playing and looks to him, as well. The place is lit with candles on the ground near bushes and trees. It seems horribly unsafe and flammable, but Timothy doesn't feel it's his place to comment. He still has his toothbrush in the hand not holding his sherry.

"Are you ready for supper, boys?" Matthew MacDonald asks of the crowd of men. They all nod. Matthew MacDonald claps his hands together and turns to Timothy. "Would you like to join us for supper?"

"Sure," Timothy answers. Matthew MacDonald grins.

"Splendid," Matthew MacDonald says. He motions to Timothy and the crowd of men, and everyone follows him through a door on the far end of the courtyard. Timothy follows for lack of any reason not to, trailing after one of the trumpet players in the band. He finishes his sherry and hands it off to the servant waiting expectantly beside him. The man takes his toothbrush and room key, as well. Timothy just lets him. He assumes he'll get them back after the whole thing is over.

Timothy enters another corridor with the men. They all trickle single-file down the shadowy hallway to another door. The hallway is only dimly lit by candles, so Timothy just focuses on the shoulders of the man in front of him to make sure he knows where he's going. Matthew MacDonald leads them into a tiny alcove, where Timothy is encouraged to remove his shoes. He does. It's just easier to go along with this sort of thing.

The next room they enter is a tremendous dining hall. The chamber is echoing with their soft footsteps. The walls are lined with mirrors, as are the floors and ceiling. The edges where each meet are lined with dark carved wood. Timothy can't make out the designs without squinting, and he's quickly distracted when he's led to the table with the rest of the guests at the hotel. He assumes. He's not sure why they're actually here. Possibly dinner theater rehearsal, if he had to guess.

"Take a seat," Matthew MacDonald tells everyone. Each man sits instantly at the seat he is closest to. There is no chair left for Timothy, so he just stands, looking around for a spot he can take. Another servant enters the room with a chair, which he brings to Matthew MacDonald. Matthew MacDonald jerks his chin in the direction of the massive table in the dead center of the room. All the chairs are situated around it, so the butler has to climb onto the table itself to haul the chair up onto the immense thing.

All the men watch silently as the butler walks across the white tablecloth and sets the chair in the center. He positions it so it's facing Matthew MacDonald, then hops off of the table and leaves the room. Matthew MacDonald makes eye contact with Timothy and motions to the chair.

"For you," Matthew MacDonald says. Timothy puts one hand on the edge of the table and hauls himself up. This is far from the strangest thing he's had to do in his lifetime.

"What kind of a company are you folks, anyways?" Timothy asks, taking the seat atop the table, facing Matthew MacDonald. "Community theater?"

"Yes," Matthew MacDonald says. It's obvious he's lying, but Timothy just looks to the man at his right instead.

"Dinner theater?" Timothy asks.

"Yes," the man says. Timothy frowns, turning to his left instead.

"Did you write this yourselves?" Timothy asks of this man. The man nods.

"Yes," he says. Timothy sighs. The butler returns, this time with four other butlers and Henry, who let Timothy into the hotel in the first place. The head butler is pushing a bar cart.

"I'm glad to see you found supper," Henry says. Timothy starts to answer, but Henry keeps speaking before he gets a chance, saying, "Is everyone ready for their serum?"

"Ambrosia," Matthew MacDonald says.

"Nectar," one of the men at the table whispers.

"Yes," another man exclaims. The five servants start pouring a silver fluid out of ancient pitchers into a plethora of glasses. From this distance, Timothy thinks they might be flutes.

Whatever this serum is that's being poured into the glasses looks like it has the consistency of mercury and the shine of venom.

The servants make quick work of the glasses, pouring and passing them out on ornate silver serving trays. Each man receives a flute and waits while Henry delivers a golden flute to Matthew MacDonald at the head of the table. The two men stand side-by-side and raise their flutes to the men. Each man raises their flute to their leaders.

"What sort of a drink is that?" Timothy asks, and is fully ignored as the men drink from their flutes. No man stops to take a breath; they drink until the flutes are empty. They lower their flutes, and each servant snatches them before they can even hit the table. Timothy watches. "Spooky. This part of the show?"

"Henry," Matthew MacDonald says. Henry snaps his fingers, and the servants leave, rolling the bar cart out of the room. They return with a different, covered serving cart. The head butler whips the lacy cover off of the cart and reveals two trays filled with knives. Timothy frowns slightly.

"What're we eating, boys?" Timothy asks.

"We're not allowed to leave," one of the men says, without precedent. Timothy glances over his shoulder, but he's not sure who spoke. The knives are distributed amongst the men. The largest blades are handed to Henry and Matthew MacDonald. They have large, ornately carved handles. They look impossible to use properly, but the two of them hold them like they already know how best to wield them.

"We meet every day," another man says.

"We are so hungry," Matthew MacDonald tells Timothy. "I'm not sure how long we've gone without a meal."

"Oh, Jesus," Timothy says, as a knife flies past his head. He jumps from the table, leaping to the floor, and the men are upon him, chasing him as he sprints for the door. The last butler to leave slams the door shut behind himself, leaving Timothy trapped in the mirrored room. There's at least a dozen men on him at once, trying to stab him, but he drops to the ground, ducking under their legs and crawling on hands and knees until he's on the other side of the crowd. Someone grabs his ankle and drags him back into the crowd.

"Don't," someone says, loudly, forcefully, and Timothy ignores them, kicking out with his stocking foot. He feels his heel connect with somebody's nose, and then there's blood splattered on his face. He jumps up again and runs for a mirror, slamming into it with all the force he can muster, shattering the glass over them in a shower of shards. He ducks, covers his face, and men cry out. They're stabbing at him still, catching his clothes, grazing his skin. He can feel blood trickling from pain points, slashes all over his body, but he just picks up a shard of glass and spins on the men.

"Back off," Timothy orders them. They don't. They keep coming at him, and he jabs at them with his shard. They're the complete opposite of the men he saw in the courtyard. Those were happy, drunk men. These are horrible, bent men; they look old and crooked, furiously angry. "What in the name of God did you drink?"

"Ambrosia," someone says.

"Nectar," says another man.

"Have you heard of Robert Louis Stevenson?" Matthew MacDonald cries from the back of the crowd. "Meet your Mr. Hydes!"

"Good Lord," Timothy says. A man slashes at him, and he darts out of the way. "You don't have to do this."

"We do!"

"It's all we have."

"Surely not," Timothy says, but a knife whizzes by his head and embeds itself in the wall behind himself, so he just grabs it by the handle, yanks it free, and wields it. "Alright, back up. I'm leaving here in one piece, boys."

"Like hell!" Henry calls. Timothy shuts one eye, aims, and whips the knife, nailing Henry right in the shoulder. Every man turns to watch Henry bite out a curse and hit the ground, grabbing at his shoulder. Timothy takes advantage of their distraction to run for the door again, breaking into a dead sprint and flinging his full weight at the old door, sending it crashing in on itself under his body weight. Servants go running as he hurtles through the alcove, through the courtyard, and back into the corridor he started in. He stops in his hotel room, the door still open, snatches up his duffle bag, and keeps running.

He can still hear men chasing after him, knives hitting the walls and floors around him, but he just keeps running through the dark corridors and lobbies and hallways and rooms until he finds a window and flings himself through it. Glass breaks around him, cutting up his forearms when he throws them up to protect his face. He crashes into a bush outside the window, rolls down the hill to his car, and digs his keys out of his duffle bag.

"You can't!" Matthew MacDonald's voice calls down to him. "Dr. Jekyll! Come back home!"

"Jesus Christ, *no,*" Timothy mutters to himself, unlocking the car. He slides into the driver's seat and peels out of the lot. He speeds away from the hotel and back onto the road, blood oozing from his skin, dripping into his lap. He gasps for breath, heinously and obviously out of shape after such a run.

Timothy drives for a bit. He's not all that tired anymore; the adrenaline's kicked in. He keeps driving, and driving, and after driving for an hour, he sees a shape looming in the distance. The sky hasn't lightened any, but he's just glad to see another sign of humanity.

The closer he gets, the more familiar the shape becomes. A shape. A building. A mansion. A hotel. Timothy stares at it, then drives past it. Possibly a horrible coincidence; someone built two odd manor hotels an hour apart in the middle of the desert.

This happens again an hour later. Then again. The next time, Timothy starts recognizing landmarks. A strange desert tree here. A peculiar bird perched on a rock there. It's all the same. It repeats, over and over. Timothy eventually pulls back into the hotel parking lot. The sky still hasn't lightened, despite the fact that it's supposed to be well past dawn. The clock in the car keeps repeating the same hour.

Timothy pops open the glove box and removes the pistol he hides in every rental car. With a sigh, he loads the thing, then climbs up and out of the car. His limbs are stiff. The car is still too small for his giant body.

"Bring it, boys!" Timothy calls, aiming a shot for one of the front windows of the hotel and firing. He hears the glass shatter, and then the front door opens. He can hear the church bells again, and the distant sounds of drums and trumpets. He fires again, and hears a squeal. A scream. He fires again.

THE DEMONS' TRIAL FOR, AND SUBSEQUENT ASSASSINATION OF, THE VILE BEAST OF AUBERBONNE

Orléans is southwest of Paris. Auberbonne is southeast of Orléans. It is in Auberbonne that Joan stops for just a night. The town is small, barely more than a collection of homes and tiny businesses, but they have space outside of town for her company to camp, and more than enough space in their homes for Joan to rest.

She accepts the offer from a kind woman, Madeleine. Madeleine's home is little more than a hovel, but Joan accepts regardless. She likes Madeleine the best of all the people in town who approach her. They have heard about her already; they knew she was coming their way. All of them want to speak with the woman who has spoken with the saints, whose arm is guided by a higher power. Being that woman, however, Joan only wants to rest.

"I don't have much to offer for food," Madeleine says. Her face is red, her expression apologetic. "I'm so sorry—"

"You are giving me a space to sleep," Joan tells her. Madeleine looks away. "Do not apologize. Not to me. Not to anyone, do you hear me? You have nothing to apologize for."

"I am not so sure," Madeleine says. Joan frowns. "I have bread and some pottage."

"What do you have to apologize for?" Joan asks. Madeleine shakes her head. "You can tell me."

"I can't," Madeleine says. "If I tell you, God and Jesus and the saints will hear me. I can't tell you."

"If you tell me, then they will all listen," Joan says. "They will believe you. They are with you. You needn't be afraid."

Madeleine looks at her. It's late; she has a small fire in her hearth, over which the pottage warms in a pot. The flames flicker, casting her face in orange shadows.

"Guillemot," Madeleine whispers. It's an unfamiliar name; Joan does not know it. "He is in charge of our town and the towns surrounding it."

"A king?" Joan asks.

"I don't know what he is," Madeleine confesses. "He takes our money and tells us how to work our land. He takes our women and beats our children."

"Has he taken you?" Joan asks. Madeleine looks away, stares into the fire. Her eyes are bloodshot. "Madeleine."

"Yes," Madeleine whispers. "And he beat my child. My son. Lorens. My boy is dead because of him." She shuts her eyes. Joan stands.

"Where does he live?" Joan asks. Madeleine bolts to her feet, grabs Joan by the wrists. They both stand still, neither sure of what to do.

"Do not go," Madeleine says. "Not even you."

"I must," Joan whispers. Madeleine shakes her head and releases Joan's wrists.

"Eat bread and pottage," Madeleine tells her. "Drink ale with me. Then, rest. Sleep. Continue on your journey tomorrow, and forget about Guillemot and Auberbonne and all these people. We live as we ought to live."

Joan knows what these people are like. She knows their fear. Her father was a peasant farmer. She nods and sits back down on the floor, watches as Madeleine bustles around her tiny home, procuring bowls and serving her pottage and her bread and her ale for the two of them to share. Joan rips off a chunk of bread and dips it in the pottage, nibbling on it.

"When do you have to be awake?" Madeleine asks. Joan lifts one shoulder in a half-shrug.

"Whenever I please," Joan says. "I tell them when to leave."

"Okay," Madeleine says. Joan leans over to her, cups her face in one hand. She strokes her thumb under Madeleine's eye, and Madeleine leans into her touch, letting Joan's palm hold up her head.

"Sleep," Joan tells her. The two of them clean up their dishes and Madeleine puts out the fire. It's a warm enough night, and the two of them climb into Madeleine's lumpy wooden bed against one wall in her home. Joan is much taller than Madeleine, stronger and larger, but Madeleine still insists on wrapping herself behind Joan, protecting her. With the covers pulled over them, they can share body heat just fine. Madeleine exhales against Joan's neck. She falls asleep first.

Joan lays awake for a long, long while. Once Madeleine is completely asleep, Joan sneaks away from her, lifting one of Madeleine's arms delicately to slip away. She lightly touches Madeleine's forehead, brushes a lock of hair away from her closed eyes, and leaves her home.

Joan's company still have a couple of fires going outside of town, camped out as they are in the low grass. Joan makes her way through them in her sleeping gown, and they all watch her go. She finds Gilles and sits beside him on the ground.

"We need to kill a man," Joan tells him.

"Consider it done," Gilles replies. He enjoys the killing. Joan shakes her head.

"No, we must do it," Joan says. "I want to be the one to do it. He's destroying this town and the neighboring villages. He's hurting the women and children."

"So?" Gilles asks. Joan turns her head to look at him, disgusted. "What?"

"You can be such a horrible man," Joan tells him. Gilles snorts and looks back at the fire.

"You just told me you want to kill a man," Gilles says. "And based on what? The word of some peasant woman? Who knows why she'd ask you to do such a thing?"

"He has a point," says Jaquet, sitting across the fire. Joan glares at him through the flames.

"I know when I hear the truth," Joan says. She stands. "His name is Guillemot. Find where he lives and where he will be tomorrow. I'll come to you in the morning."

"What about our journey?" Jaquet asks. Joan looks away from him.

"Delay it one day," Joan tells him.

"For what?" Jaquet snorts. Joan doesn't look back.

"For them, you animal," Joan says, and leaves, walking towards the edge of the woods, far from the town, far from the campsite. She slips beyond the first trees and finds herself a heavy, wide rock to sit on, laying across a flat spot atop the thing. The woods aren't empty; they are filled with animals and insects and plants and breezes. Joan hears the crack of a twig being stepped on and broken in half, and she turns her head against the rock to look at the source of the sound.

"Hello, Margaret," Joan says, putting her hand over her eyes. Saint Margaret stands before her; Saint Michael and Saint Catherine lag behind. "What news have you for me today?"

"You are on a holy quest," Margaret tells her. "You are right to kill this man."

Joan glances at her again. "You're saying I should kill?"

"You should," Michael insists. "You must. You have to kill Guillemot. He deserves to die."

Joan frowns, sitting up on the rock. She looks to Saint Catherine, who shrugs. "He deserves to die?"

"All humans deserve to die," Catherine says. Michael pulls his sword from his belt and weighs it between his hands.

The woods seem quiet with the three of them there. All animals go still, all insects fall to the Earth. The breeze is stifled. The plants hold their breath.

"I know what it is to die," Catherine tells her. She removes the crown from her head and holds it out to Joan. Joan takes it; it pricks her fingers, unexpectedly sharp at its edges. "It is no small feat. But it is your final goal."

"For myself?" Joan asks.

"For all," Margaret says. "For all people. It is your duty to bring them to us."

"To kill?" Joan asks, passing the crown back. Margaret steps forward, removes the black cross from around her neck. The cross dangles upside-down as she hangs it around Joan's throat.

"Yes," Margaret says. She backs away and motions Michael forward.

"Names are interchangeable," Michael says, apropos of nothing. He takes a couple of steps towards Joan. "Hold out your hands."

Joan does. She stares at the three of them.

"You are saints," Joan says, but it's pitched like a question. They don't look at each other; they keep staring at Joan. "You *are* saints, aren't you?"

"No," Michael says. "We were angels."

"We have fallen," Margaret says.

"All must fall," Catherine adds.

"Including man," Michael finishes. He slashes the sword across Joan's palms, slicing her skin open. She flinches, but keeps her hands steady, holding them out still. Michael stares at the blood dripping to the ground.

"Angels and demons and saints and sinners are all the same," Michael says. "We are martyrs. You will be a martyr."

"I will?" Joan asks. She curls her fingers around her bleeding hands.

"You have to be," Catherine tells her. She places her crown on Joan's head. Joan just bows her head to accept it. "There's nothing else for you to be."

"You will die," Margaret says. "You will join us. You must. But it is a pleasant occupation."

Joan stares at them, then glances down at the blood dripping onto her feet. She withdraws her hands and places them in her lap. The blood puddles in the caught material of her nightgown, a bowl in her lap.

"I want to serve God," Joan says.

"There isn't one God," Michael insists. "There are many options. It isn't who you choose, it's what you believe."

"There's someone for everyone," Catherine says. "You can take your pick."

"How do I know I'm making the right choice?" Joan asks.

"You don't," Margaret says, and the three of them vanish. They leave Joan sitting on her rock, blood streaming down her arms, and the woods come back to life the moment they're gone. The animals and insects spring back into the air, return to the world of the waking and living. The breeze lifts Joan's short hair off of her neck. The Earth hums and sings to her. She is briefly blinded by a white light, and she closes her eyes against it. When she lifts her bleeding hands, the crown is gone from her head; she only succeeds in smearing blood on her face and in her hair.

Joan stands and finds that it is daytime. Dawn has come in no time at all. She leaves the woods, strides past the campsite, and marches right back into town, into Madeleine's home. Madeleine is still asleep, and Joan leans over her, nudges her with her clean elbow.

"Madeleine," Joan whispers, and Madeleine's eyes blink open. She immediately frowns, sitting up abruptly.

"You're hurt," Madeleine says. She drags herself out of bed.

"I had a vision," Joan says, and recounts the whole thing to Madeleine as Madeleine cleans and wraps her hands and washes her face and hair. Madeleine nods in all the right places and hums her agreements and listens to the entire story.

"Are they saints?" Madeleine asks. Joan shakes her head.

"I don't know," Joan says. "But they are holy, and they require my service."

"Then you must give it," Madeleine tells her. Joan kisses her on the cheek, and Madeleine sighs.

"I will kill Guillemot today," Joan tells her. "I must. I was ordered to kill him and my men will help me."

"Thank you," Madeleine says. She has tears in her eyes. "Thank you, Joan."

"It is for us all that I do this," Joan says. She rises from the floor and returns to Gilles, who is already dressed and ready to depart. He gives her her armor. He tells her that he knows where Guillemot lives, and Joan leads her company to the house.

It is as near to a manor home as these villages will ever see. The villagers and townspeople follow, morbidly curious and cautiously optimistic.

Joan has Gilles kick down the door. She doesn't even need to enter the home; Guillemot walks outside of his own accord.

"Guillemot d'Auberbonne," Joan announces. Guillemot squints at her, clearly just having woken up. He has a sword in one hand. Joan's hands are still oozing blood, but she wears her plate armor. Gilles hands her her crossbow and bolts. "You are being punished."

"For what?" Guillemot asks. Joan lifts her crossbow and aims between his eyes.

"For your crimes against these people," Joan says. Guillemot looks past her and sees the villagers behind her company.

"I'm their king," Guillemot says. "I am their leader. They need somebody like me. They don't know what to do *without* me. They're towns filled with idiots and fools and I am the only one who can guide them."

"You rape and beat and murder them," Joan says.

"They deserve it," Guillemot tells her. Joan fires her bolt into his forehead, and he hits the ground, dead before his back is in the dirt. Joan hands her crossbow back to Gilles and turns to the crowd of soldiers and villagers and children and townspeople.

"The Devil is in this woman," one of the men from the town shouts.

"No!" Madeleine calls. "It is God!"

"It is me," Joan tells them all. "I make my own decisions and I speak with saints and demons and I know what men are. I know who I am in relation to all of this." Joan looks up at the sky, and the sun blinds her eyes. She shuts them, lets her eyelids protect her. She hears people going to the body of Guillemot.

She hears people murmuring to each other. They fall silent when she opens her mouth again. "I am divine."

ALL THE WAY DOWN

how it begins is this:

i take a length of braided rope,

snap it for strength,

and tie a noose into it;

then, i hold it up,

making sure it's the size of my head

i drape it over the back of the sofa

and stand far back:

i hold a quarter up to my eye

and slide it into the hollow

and think, yes,

these are the same little circles

i take my rope outside

to join me in the tallest tree

at the end of my block,

where i climb to the highest branch

scoot out to the edge

and take my chances.

there is nothing for me here.

i want the world to die with me.

i want to cosmically disrupt our orbit

and smash my world to pieces,

a mass extinction event,

cretaceous–paleogene,

shattering through me,

the new chicxulub crater

i lasso the rope,

i scoop the knot,

and i toss the braid to the sky,

where it flies for miles and miles

until it slides around the moon

and i give her a sharp tug

i wonder if this is how the yucatán felt

on impact

and in my last moment, i think,

i am so glad she hurdled at me,

the destroyer,

in a blaze of moonlight, 2:47am

WE WHO STAND TOGETHER

Despite all odds, Avery loves taking care of the plants in the gardening center at the Home Improvement Warehouse. She loves it enough to stay late nearly every day, distracted by it. She doesn't have anyone to go home to, really, anyways, so it doesn't matter so much if she stays. There isn't much to do at home except eat cereal, look after her own plants, and watch television.

Avery leaves work late, again. She's the last one to leave, so she locks and arms the building, popping in her headphones as she taps out the keycode. She looks out at the bus stop across the street, how dimly lit it is, how empty it seems. She takes her headphones back out and jogs to it.

No bus comes for a while, long enough that she starts to get antsy. By the time it does show its face, she's one of the only people on it. She stares out the window, watching haphazardly-parked cars and evenly-placed sidewalk trees and apartment complexes flick by. She thinks she sees a weird streak of silver light, maybe, but when she blinks, it's gone. She thinks, *maybe it was a grocery store,* and forgets about it.

She sees another silver streak when she gets off the bus, but it's nearer to the woods now. *Probably the headlights of the bus,* she thinks. She keeps her keys between her fingers regardless as she walks quickly to her house, unable to stop herself from feeling heart-pounding anxiety despite the fact that the streets seem empty.

Her apartment, too, seems empty. This isn't strange, though; she'd be more upset if someone actually was inside. She shuts the door behind herself, and she's only a couple of steps up her front staircase when there is a knock on her door. Frowning, she peeks through the peephole. There's a man on the other side; he's old, tired-looking, greying black hair and drooping eyes and fidgeting movements. She doesn't say anything, doesn't move, holds her breath.

"Hello?" the man calls. Her pulse speeds up. "Hello, I— Sorry, I saw you go into your apartment, and I need help. I got locked out of my building, I'm right next door to you, nobody else is answering their doors. I left my phone inside my place and I need to make a call, and every place is closed. Can you help?"

Avery still doesn't open the door, still doesn't move, still doesn't answer. She just keeps watching the guy through the peephole.

"Jesus Christ," she hears the guy mutter, as she watches him scuff his feet on her front steps. "People have no fucking common decency these days."

Avery watches the man crouch down slightly, and then a hand comes through her mail slot, reaching for anything it could find, fingers groping for purchase. She flattens herself against the wall, slamming her hand over her mouth, heart pounding, eyes tearing up, trying not to make any noise. His hand catches her skirt, and she screams, finally, shoving his hand away and sprinting up the stairs. She doesn't stop to look backwards, but she hears a *crack* and a *crash* as her door is forced in. She slides around the corner, barely making it to the other side of her kitchen before she hears the man hit the top of her stairs.

"Don't!" she screams, grabbing a knife from the block on the counter and holding it out. "God, don't, please don't, please don't hurt me—"

The man doesn't even say anything, just sprints at her faster than she's ever seen anyone move before. She slashes at him with the knife and catches his face, blade slicing through his cheek. He grabs her wrists and squeezes until she drops the knife.

"Stop," he says. "Come here."

He drags Avery into a tight embrace, ignoring her as she sobs and shoves at him. He just brings her wrist to his mouth and bites her.

"What are you doing?" she demands. He doesn't answer, apparently now *sucking* at her wrist. "Jesus Chr— What are you *doing?*"

"Shut up," he spits, affixing his mouth to the open wound on her wrist. She punches at his chest again, but she feels the blood pulsing out of her, feels the energy leaving her. She desperately tries to stay awake, terrified of what could happen if she loses consciousness, but she can't stop it. She blinks, and blinks again, hands moving like they're underwater. She slumps, and he catches her, and she is out.

She wakes up on her kitchen floor, and the first thing she sees is a knife on the tile in front of her. She drags herself up, propped up on her elbow, and looks around, but sees no one else. She can still see blood smeared on her wrist, but the wound she had seen the stranger rip open with his teeth isn't there. She touches the thin skin lightly with her fingertips, prods at it, but— no, nothing.

She takes up the knife and hauls herself to her feet. She forces herself not to think of anything, not anything but searching her apartment for the stranger. There's no one. No one in the closets, no one under the sink, no one behind the shower curtain, no one anywhere. She is completely and utterly alone.

Avery realizes, upon pulling her phone out of her bag, that she has no one to call. She could call the police, but both the man and her wounds are gone now, so they probably wouldn't even believe her if she *did* call, let alone *help* her. She doesn't have many close friends in the city, if any, and nobody in her family would care. Acquaintances, coworkers, neighbors — it's nothing they should be bothered with from her.

The bedroom is empty when she checks it for the third time. She leaves it there, instead goes to make sure every door and window is shut, locked, and bolted, going to the lengths to drag chairs in front of every door. Her front door, despite the fact that she heard it get broken, is fixed now, on its hinges once again. She closes, locks, bolts, and barricades it. After a moment of consideration, she duct-tapes the peephole closed and the mail slot shut.

With everything closed, every blind down, every curtain drawn, Avery returns to her bedroom one last time. She leaves the knife on her bedside table, climbs into bed.

She stares at the wall.

She can't stop her brain. She can't quiet her mind, and yet she's not really thinking anything; there's just a humming buzz filling the space in her head.

When the sun comes up, she still hasn't slept. One ray of sunshine sneaks through her curtains, landing directly on her left eye, burning her. She flinches, slamming her eyes shut, yanking the covers up over her head and hiding under them.

Avery wakes up again at dusk. She can sense immediately from the lighting that it's after seven o'clock, at least, but she lays in bed for a while before getting up for food. Nothing in her kitchen is appetizing, but Avery is *starving*. She hates standing on the cold tile, because the kitchen haunts her; in her peripheral vision, the stranger is in every corner, so she grits her teeth, grabs a box of crackers, and retreats to her bedroom once more.

Only three crackers later, she feels sick. She stops, tries to process what she's feeling, and only seconds later she's vomiting onto the floor. She gets up to clean it, then sits on the floor, unable to find the energy or desire to get back onto the bed.

She spends the next four days in essentially the same way. She calls out of work for every shift. She sleeps all day, lies awake all night. She's starving, but everything she tries to eat makes her sick. Five days later, on Friday, she's laying in her bed, almost certain that she's dying. She just doesn't know why.

Avery is dehydrated; she hasn't kept anything down in nearly a week. She's exhausted. Her energy is gone. No one has come to check up on her. She's almost certain she should be in a hospital, but she can't get herself there, and couldn't afford it if she did. That night, she resigns herself. She'll die if she keeps going. She knows she needs a doctor, so she heaves herself out of bed, searches directions to an all-night free clinic on her phone, and stands in the middle of the kitchen.

The stairs down to her barricaded front door taunt her: shadowed, containing god-knows-what in the darkness. She puts a knife in her purse, and another in her pocket. She puts an old container of pepper spray in her bra. Armed to (and including) the teeth, she braves the stairs, uncovers her front door, and leaves.

It's warm outside, but Avery's freezing. Her fingers are stiff and her hands have paled to an unfamiliar, ghostly tan. She lets her lank, dark hair fall forward to hide her face, and she shuffles down the street that way. The lights of the moon and of the fluorescent street lights guide her path. It's slow-going, and she stops when she hears a footstep hit the sidewalk behind her.

Avery slows, glancing back over her shoulder at the man behind her. Suddenly, abruptly, in a wave of heat, she's *hungry,* and she finds herself staring at the man as he passes by her. He gives her a strange look, but she forgets to be afraid in the face of her overwhelming desire to bite into the man's flesh.

The man leaves with his life, unaware of how close he was to losing it. Avery takes a gasping breath once he's gone, baffled and terrified by herself. She tries to keep heading for the clinic, but another man rounds the corner, and she feels that same strange urge again. She forces herself to duck down an empty alley, sitting on the filthy ground beside a dumpster, heart pounding. She rests her head against the side of the dumpster and tries to catch her breath, but she can't.

"Shit," she hisses, voice no more than a whisper. She lifts her trembling hands and fumbles for the racing pulse in her throat. She squeezes her eyes shut, feels her breath catch in her throat, and true terror takes over. The concept of death is abruptly too final, too solid, too real, too much, and her hands go to her mouth as she gasps on a sob.

"Oh, my God," someone's soft voice says above her. Avery squints her eyes up to see who found her, but can't gather the strength to stand up. She sees a pretty white face, heavy brown eyebrows pulled together in concern, but that's all the sees before she closes her eyes again.

"Please help me," she says, because it's the only option she has left. There are hands on her abruptly, unexpectedly, and she flinches away.

"You're okay, I've got you," the woman says. "Can I touch you?"

"Yeah, sorry," Avery says. The woman touches her again, but Avery doesn't flinch this time. The hands pull her away from the dumpster and guide her down into the woman's lap.

"Don't apologize," the woman says. "You've been through so much. Who did this to you?"

"I don't know," Avery says. "I— A man broke in. I didn't know him. I don't know what he did to me."

"Oh, baby," the woman says softly. "It's almost over. You're almost there."

"Almost where?" Avery asks. The woman strokes Avery's hair back from her face, so Avery forces her eyes open to look at her again.

"The other side," the woman says, haloed by dingy street lights.

"That's so dramatic," Avery whispers. The woman huffs a laugh. "Am I gonna die?"

"Not quite," the woman tells her. "But it's the closest we'll ever get."

"What the fuck does that mean?" Avery asks, but the woman is looking away now, talking to someone else in the alley too quickly for Avery to process the words. "Who is that? Who are you?"

"My name is Harriet," the woman says. Avery nods. "This is Patience."

"Hello," another voice says. Avery opens her eyes again, even if she doesn't remember closing them, and sees a small, fine face looking down at her. "You're going to be okay. The man who attacked you, did he bite you?"

"Yeah," Avery tells her. She frowns, furrows her brow, tries to sit up. She can't. Harriet holds onto her. "Why?"

"He's transformed her already," Patience says to Harriet. "We can't complete it ourselves."

"We can help her through it, though," Harriet says. The two of them stare at each other for a moment.

"Help me through what?" Avery asks. Harriet looks to her, but Patience just stands up and turns away.

"He turned you," Harriet tells her. "How much do you know about vampires?"

Avery stares up at her. A long moment of silence passes before she says, "Oh, this is a *bad* goddamn dream."

"It's not—"

"I definitely passed out or something at my house and this is just a weird dream," Avery says. She tries to shove away from Harriet again, but she can't get enough strength to move. "Oh, fuck, it's just a dream—"

"It's not a dream," Harriet insists. "What's your name?"

"Avery," Avery says. It's a dream, so why not tell the truth? Nothing even matters anyways.

"Avery, this is not a dream," Harriet tells her. "It's not. I promise you. But I'm going to help you through this. I'm going to bring you back to my house to recover. Can you stand?"

"Oh, Jesus," Avery groans, half-laughing. "Never go to a second location, Harriet."

Harriet smiles again, just a little bit. "Is it okay if we go back to my house?"

Avery thinks of the sterile clinic, then of her empty apartment, and she looks up into Harriet's face. *Better than nothing.* "Yeah, that's okay."

"Okay," Harriet agrees. She lifts her head. "Patience, help me lift her up, please."

"We should bring her back to the others," Patience says, as she goes to Avery's other side and helps her to her feet. Avery is unsteady, so Harriet just reaches around and pulls her arm across her shoulders, holding most of Avery's weight up so she doesn't topple over.

"The other vampires?" Avery asks. "Do I have to, like— Are you gonna make me sleep in a coffin? I'm a little claustrophobic."

"You just have to be in the darkness when the sun comes up," Harriet says. "We won't make you sleep in a coffin. Unless you want to."

"Hattie," Patience says, sounding playfully admonishing. Avery tilts her head to look at her.

"Who am I to judge? Everyone does things their own way," Harriet replies. She hoists Avery up so her knees are a little sturdier. "Come on, we're going to bring you home. Close your eyes for me, okay?"

"Can do," Avery tells her, and her eyes slip shut easily. She feels wind hitting her in the face, and she coughs, but she keeps her eyes shut. At this point, really, nothing matters; either it's a dream and she'll wake up, or it's not a dream and she'll die anyways. Either way, this is pretty much out of her hands at this point.

"Open your eyes," Patience says. Avery blinks, then squints.

"Where the hell am I?" Avery asks, because it's only been about fifteen seconds but she's not in the alley anymore. Instead, she's standing on someone's front lawn, in the dark, staring up at an enormous old yellow house. She glances around and sees trees, and a garden, and behind her there's an empty road.

"This is where we live," Harriet says.

"We as in, just you two guys??" Avery asks. "Or we as in, like, a gang of vampires?"

"I wouldn't call them a gang," Harriet replies. Avery groans, leaning against Harriet's side. She can feel her heartbeat slowing down, which would be more reassuring if it wasn't slowing to a glacially sluggish pace. "They're more of a... Well, what are we, Patience?"

"A nest?" Patience suggests. "That's what they used to call us."

"That sounds stupid," Harriet says. Patience laughs. "A coven?"

"That's witches," Avery tells her. Harriet glances down at her. "Witches have covens."

"We could have a coven," Harriet tells her, smiling. " "More of a... I don't know what the word would be."

"We used to call them clans," Patience says. "Or broods." Harriet groans.

"That's *so* outdated," Harriet tells her.

"A clutch?" Avery suggests. Harriet glances to Patience, smiling.

"We don't call them clutches anymore," Patience says.

"Oh, I'm *so sorry,*" Avery says. Harriet laughs, this time. "I didn't know there were new and separate names. A murder of crows, a coven of witches, a nest of vampires... whatever, *whatever!*"

"I kinda like *coven,*" Harriet says. "I think I'm gonna use that."

"What the hell is going on out there?" someone shouts from one of the windows at the front of the house. "Who— Oh, God, who *is* that? She looks like death."

"That's because she's dying," Harriet deadpans back. Patience rubs Avery's back when Avery feels tears come unexpectedly into her eyes. Harriet glances down at her, then says, "Oh, shit, I'm sorry. You're not actually dying. Your human form is dying to make way for your immortal form."

"That's so much fucking worse," Avery replies. Harriet strokes Avery's hair back from her face, then cups her cheek for a moment, looking into her eyes.

"It's almost over," Harriet says. She turns back to the window. "Bunny, get down here, help us get her inside."

Avery hears the front door slam open, and then there's someone standing in front of her, presumably Bunny. The tall woman leans down into Avery's face and grins at her.

"Hey there," Bunny says. "Who are you?"

"Her name is Avery and she needs to lie down," Harriet tells her. Bunny ducks down, scoops Avery up into her arms, and takes off into the house. Avery just holds onto her, half-frightened, half-interested. Bunny gently lays her down on a huge sofa, shoving a pillow under her head and then kneeling on the floor beside her.

"What happened?" Bunny asks.

299

"We—" Harriet starts to say, but Bunny waves her off, not taking her eyes off of Avery. Avery can't help but stare back at her. Bunny is beautiful, to understate her; she's got short, dark hair curling back from her face, thin eyes, full lips, identical eyebrows. Avery can't stop staring at her. Despite the hour, she's still fully-dressed in a bespoke suit, and all of her attention is focused on Avery.

"I asked her," Bunny says. She glances back at Harriet. "I know you wanna help, but she has to want to help herself, too." Bunny looks down at Avery, looks her over before landing her attention back at her face, on her eyes. "What happened to you?"

Avery glances at Harriet over Bunny's shoulder, and Patience behind her. Neither of them says anything, so Avery looks back to Bunny, and she tells her *everything*. It just all pours out of her; the man who followed her, how he broke into her apartment, what he did to her. She tells Bunny about the last week, about feeling like she's been slowly dying, about not really *caring* because she didn't even want to get out of bed. While she talks, Bunny takes her hand, holds it tight, nods encouragingly in all the right places.

"And then I figured, I didn't really want to die alone," Avery says, "so I tried to get to a clinic or something, but when I was walking, I—" She stops, because she doesn't know how to describe how she felt. "I kind of wanted— As soon as I saw someone, I just—"

"I know," Bunny says. She squeezes Avery's hand. "You're starting to transform. I know it's scary, and I'm sorry. You're gonna be fine, though, I can tell. Right?"

"Sure," Avery says. "It sounds like bullshit."

Bunny laughs. "I said the same thing, you know. I didn't believe in, like, *any* of it. Some of it's still stupid. Like, ghosts aren't real—"

"Ghosts *are real,*" Harriet says behind her, but Bunny keeps talking like she wasn't interrupted.

"—but this *is* real," Bunny says. She strokes Avery's hair back from her face. "This is real, and you're going to be okay. I'll stay here with you the whole time. Alright?"

"Okay," Avery says, softly. Her heartbeat is still slowing down, and she figures, if she *does* die, at least she isn't actually dying alone. These people might be strangers, but at least they're people.

"Hattie, will you go tell the others to stay out of here for the time being?" Patience asks. Harriet nods and leaves the room, moving more quickly than Avery has ever seen someone move. Patience comes to stand beside Bunny. She does not kneel, but she does place a hand over Avery's forehead and eyes. Avery shuts her eyes under the cold skin.

"She's nearly there," Patience says. She lifts her hand, and Avery blinks her eyes open again. "Call for me if you need me. I'll ask Murphy to sit in the next room and listen for you."

"Thank you," Bunny says. Patience glances at Avery, then takes one knee, turning her face away to speak only to Bunny.

"This is unlike you," Patience says, softly. Avery pretends not to be listening, staring up at the ceiling and focusing on her own slowing pulse. It's not hard to act distracted by the fact that she's probably fucking dying on this lady's couch.

"She needs help," Bunny whispers back. "I just— I don't know what it is. She needs *my* help."

There's a beat of silence. Then, Patience stands up again.

"Be careful," Patience says, and she leaves. Avery looks back down at Bunny.

"What, are you usually a jackass?" Avery asks, and Bunny snorts a laugh.

"You're not actually far off," Bunny says. "I'm kind of a jackass."

"Well, take it from me," Avery tells her, "you're not all that bad."

Bunny squeezes her hand in response, but doesn't say anything.

"So, when I'm a vampire," Avery asks, "do I have to go around hypnotizing people and drinking their blood? Or, like, am I gonna have to move into a castle, or something? I heard talk of coffin beds—"

"Oh, God," Bunny says, laughing. "Jesus, no, you don't have to do any of that. I mean, blood-drinking, actually, yes—"

"That was the literal worst one," Avery says. "You said I have to do the *worst one*. Also, can you say 'God' and 'Jesus'? Aren't vampires demons?"

"No, we're just different kinds of humans," Bunny tells her. Avery snorts.

"Humans who eat other humans," Avery says.

"That's cannibalism," Bunny corrects her. "Vampirism is just the blood. You don't have to eat them."

"If you insist," Avery replies. Bunny laughs again, and Avery looks at her, rolling her head on the pillow, unable to lift her head or move her neck. "Am I going to die?"

"No," Bunny says, without hesitation. "When I was— I went through the same thing. I didn't believe it. Patience found me, too. Well, Jessica found me, and Patty showed up. I thought I was dying, and Patty told me I was gonna turn into a vampire, and I think I literally died saying *that's bullshit!*"

"But you died?" Avery asks. Bunny takes a second, then shakes her head.

"I said died, but it's like… I don't know." Bunny runs her free hand through her hair. "It's a transformation. It's like, puberty in two minutes."

"That's horrible," Avery says. Bunny laughs.

"It doesn't *feel* like that," Bunny says. "It's just what it's like. A total transformation from what you were into what you are. Or, in your case, will be."

"It feels bad," Avery tells her. Bunny nods.

"Understatement of the century," Bunny says. "It feels really bad. I'll be right here, though. Alright? The whole time."

"Okay," Avery says. She hesitates for a second, then says, softly, "Please don't let go."

"I won't," Bunny tells her, and it's the last thing Avery hears before her heart stops.

Avery's whole life doesn't flash before her eyes, like she assumed it would. Instead, in this moment, she can only think of everything she *didn't* get to do, and it's even worse. It's cruel, in a way, because regardless of what Bunny said, she's pretty sure she's going to die, and there's so much she hasn't gotten to do. She tells herself that, if she *does* live, she'll do a little more. Try and embrace some of those things she's thinking about, so she doesn't waste anymore time.

It hurts, for a little while, and then it doesn't. Then it's more like she's underwater, and she can't feel or see anything, but she can think, distantly. Her thoughts are disordered; she can't hold onto any one concept before it floats away. Awareness comes back to her in pieces; things are cold, and they ache, and she forces herself through it because she thinks she might just survive this if she does.

She wakes up again, and it's still dark, and Bunny is still there, looking slightly harrowed. When she sees Avery's eyes open, though, she smiles.

"You're a loud screamer," Bunny says.

"You don't know the half of it," Avery replies, without a second thought. Everything seems loud. "I didn't even know I was screaming. Sorry."

"Dying is scary," Bunny tells her. "You're allowed to scream."

Avery doesn't hurt anymore. The illness that's been weighing on her for days is suddenly lifted, suddenly gone. She sits up on her own, then lifts her hand, tapping her teeth with her fingertips. She runs the pad of her index finger over one sharp canine tooth. It *definitely* wasn't that sharp before. She looks to Bunny.

"This feels… better," Avery says, almost questioning how she feels. "Do I have to eat people now?"

"Like I said," Bunny repeats, "we don't eat people. But you have to drink blood, yeah. You have to drink a vampire's blood first. It completes the process. Most of us drank Patty's blood, if you want me to get her."

Avery stares at her. "Does that make her our, like, vampire mother? Or something?"

"No, that's just because she's Patty," Bunny says. "It connects you to the person but doesn't give either of you an obligation or anything. It's just the last piece."

Avery keeps staring, then looks away. She doesn't know how to ask, but Bunny seems to be able to read it in her face anyways.

"What is it?" Bunny asks. "You don't want her to do it?"

"Can you do it?" Avery asks. It's not because she doesn't like Patience, because she does. Her and Harriet seem like wonderful people. But since apparently this is all somehow real, and she is alive, and she is a vampire — Bunny's the one who took her through it. It kind of feels better to ask her to do it.

Bunny's looking back at her when Avery glances up. "I've never done it before."

"It's okay if you—"

"I want to," Bunny says. She hesitates for a second, then lifts her wrist up. She bites into the flesh below her palm and holds out her arm. Avery doesn't move. "Go ahead."

"It's still weird," Avery tells her. Bunny nods.

"Yeah, I know," she says, and something in her tone says she really *does* know, so Avery lets Bunny press her wrist to her lips and she drinks from her.

"I can take you out," Bunny says. "I want to. I'll train you myself. You don't have to stay with us, but if you want to, I can do that."

Avery doesn't answer right away. She waits until after Bunny has pulled her arm back and wrapped her hand around the bleeding wound to say, "Okay."

"Do you have anyone you want to call?" Bunny asks, and Avery thinks, but nobody springs to mind immediately, so she shakes her head. "Okay. Do you want to meet everyone else?"

"Sure," Avery says. "Should I, like— Should I know anything? Is anyone gonna hate me?"

"Absolutely not," Bunny tells her. "Abso*lutely* not." She lifts her head and calls, "Hey, Murphy!"

A young woman with dark hair, dark skin, dark eyes, and a bright purple nightgown on, sticks her head into the room. "Did she make it?"

"She did," Bunny says. She stands and offers Avery a hand, and Avery takes it, standing up on shaky legs. Everything feels loud, and bright, and crisp. She almost topples over with the rush of it, but Bunny holds on tight, and she doesn't fall. "Wanna call everyone else together? She wants to introduce herself."

Avery formally meets Murphy, who's quiet but very warm and kind, and her partner, Jessica, a short woman who shakes Avery's hand vigorously and tells her she's so excited to have her here. She meets Theresa next, and her daughter, Penelope, who introduces herself as Penny. They look nearly the same, and act nearly the same: exuberant, happy to be here. Theresa transformed first, and Penny asked to be changed when she reached the same age, apparently, when Bunny explains the situation to Avery. The last woman is Lupe, who's a little shy when she introduces herself.

"She was the last one to join us," Patience says. "We found her about... oh, how long ago was it, Lupe?"

"Almost seventy-five years," Lupe tells her. Patience smiles at her.

"What, you haven't seen anyone new in seventy-five years?" Avery asks.

"We have," Bunny says. "They just usually don't stick around long. There was Sylvia, and Alex—"

"And Helen," Penny chimes in.

"Oh, yeah, Helen." Bunny smiles at Avery. "Not everyone chooses to stay. Some want to explore. Some want to return to their normal lives."

"As normal as they can be," Theresa says.

"Close enough," Bunny allows. "So, we see them, now and then. They just don't stay to live with us."

"Do you want me to live with you?" Avery asks.

"That's your choice," Patience says. "You may do whatever you want, but you're welcome here if you wish to stay."

"Either way, I'll help you," Bunny tells her. Avery thinks about it for— honestly, not very long. She's always been both impulsive and lonely.

"I want to stay," Avery says. "For now."

Bunny smiles at her again. Avery looks at the women of the house and thinks, *Well, if it's a fever dream, hopefully I won't wake up.*

———

It's not a fever dream. Avery moves into the house, and finds out more about the women. Patience has been saving women for years after they're turned and abandoned by men. She considers them all sisters and daughters. She's strong, quiet, and hovers around the peripherals a lot, but she'll sit around the fireplace with them at night and listen to them talk. Avery respects her for it.

The women of the coven do exactly what Bunny said they'd do: they train her. They teach her to hunt without getting caught. Bunny and Avery spend most nights out in the city, cornering people in alleyways, taking just enough blood to send them on their way, unsure of what happened, still alive, still human, still safe.

They also teach her to fight. She's prepared should anyone attack her, or if a vampire hunter finds her. She laughs when she hears vampire hunters exist, but the more she thinks about it, the more unsettled she is by the concept of a man whose sole job is to kill her. She trains with the women — again, mostly with Bunny.

She learns to protect herself. She learns to hide. She learns to lead a normal life, and finds out that most of these women have jobs. Bunny works in an all-night diner; Murphy is a nighttime security guard in a museum. Avery takes night shifts at a National Park nearby, tending to their gardens and their nocturnal blooms. It's a nice way to keep herself busy, and to keep herself feeling human.

Bunny takes Avery under her wing. She spends most of her time with Avery, training her, helping her hunt, helping her fight. Sometimes she shows up in the gardens at work. Sometimes Avery visits her at the diner. Sometimes they just sit alone together on the roof balcony of the old yellow house, staring at the moon.

"Why can we be out at night and not during the day?" Avery asks, one night, when they're sitting side-by-side on the balcony. Their legs are dangling over the edge, through the railing posts, into open air.

"Because of the sunlight," Bunny tells her.

"But moonlight is just reflected sunlight," Avery argues, and Bunny kisses her. It's the first time she kisses her, but it's not the last, not by far.

Avery is happy in the yellow house. She's happy with these women. She gets along well with all of them, and they seem to like her. They even start getting used to her, and she gets used to them, and she feels comfortable and liked and content, for the first time in a long time. It's weird that it took becoming a goddamn vampire to get there, but, whatever works.

The vampire thing doesn't bother Avery as much as the becoming-a-vampire thing does. She thinks about the man who broke into her house more often than not. She searches for him every night she's out. She's told Bunny that she wants to kill him, but she's not sure if she can do it. She means it, but she's not sure how capable she is of killing.

———

Four months later, she finds out how capable she is.

Avery and Bunny are out hunting, like they usually are around one o'clock, when Avery smells something familiar. All of her senses are enhanced, as a vampire, and she knows to follow her instincts, so she changes course and follows the scent. She can't quite place it, isn't quite sure what it is, but Bunny follows her anyways.

They come to an alleyway that's nearly empty, save for a woman hiding in a ball behind a dumpster, and a man standing in front of her, in the action of grabbing her wrist when Avery sees them.

She recognizes him instantly.

"You," she says, and all the training she's been going through kicks in after a moment of hesitation. She sprints at him, punches him across the face without any style or finesse. His head snaps back, and she sweeps him out at the knees, knocking him to the ground. She can hear Bunny behind her, talking softly to the woman crouched on the ground, but she ignores them in favor of pinning the man to the ground.

It's him, is all Avery can think, over and over again, as she places her knees on his chest and uses her weight to hold him down. It's the same man who broke into her apartment, who attacked her and left her for dead, or for— vampirism, whichever's worse. The man who violated her, took everything from her.

"Fuck you," she spits, as she gets her hands on either side of his head and *twists,* ripping it from his neck. She holds it up, blood spilling out everywhere like an upturned bucket, the hole in his neck like a fire hose.

"Jesus goddamn Christ," Bunny says. Avery turns back to her, still holding the head, and briefly feels bad when she sees the look on the stranger's face. Bunny looks down at her, cups the woman's face in her hands, and says, "You didn't see anything. This was a bad dream. Go home, go to sleep, and forget about this in the morning."

The woman nods, stiffly stands, and walks out of the alley, robotic. Bunny turns to Avery, who's still just sitting there.

She slid off of the body to sit beside it, holding his severed head in her lap.

"Avery?" Bunny says, cautiously, hesitant. Avery looks up at her and isn't sure how she's feeling. "Are you okay?"

"I don't know," Avery admits.

"Was that him?" Bunny asks. She doesn't need to clarify who she means; Avery nods. "Okay. Will you give me that?" She points at the head. Avery holds it out, and Bunny takes it by the hair, taking it back to the neck and placing it down.

"I don't want to tell them," Avery says. Bunny glances back at her. "Patty and the rest. I don't want them to know that I—" Avery can't finish. She doesn't want to say it. She doesn't even know what she means to say.

"It's okay," Bunny says. She sits down next to Avery, pulls her head close and strokes her hair, drags her into her lap and holds her. Avery lets her, shutting her eyes and trying to even out her breathing. She doesn't even need to breathe, but it helps.

"They'll all understand," Bunny says, eventually. "It's kind of— I mean, it's our goal. Vengeance."

"What?" Avery asks. Bunny looks down at her, and Avery tips her head back for eye contact. "What does that mean?"

"Why do you think we've been training you to fight?" Bunny asks. Avery realizes she never really asked.

"Oh," she says.

"Yeah," Bunny says. "Most of the women we help leave after they kill whichever dick attacked them. It's our whole thing."

"I don't wanna leave," Avery tells her.

"You don't have to." Bunny strokes her hair again. "I'm gonna call Patience, though, okay? She can help us get rid of him."

"Okay," Avery agrees. Bunny pulls her phone out and calls the house. She doesn't let go of Avery; not when the rest of the coven arrives, not when they bundle the guy's dead body into a duffle bag, not when they bring the duffle bag to a clearing in the woods of a neighboring town and burn him. Patience comes to stand next to Avery as the smoke fills the air and their unmoving lungs.

"What do you want to do now, Avery?" Patience asks. All eyes are on her. Bunny's hand is cold in hers, but they feel warm, from the proximity to the fire. The flame-lights flicker on everyone's faces, the faces of the women who helped her kill and destroy the man who tried to take everything from her.

"I want to stay with you," Avery says. "I just— I don't think I'm over it yet."

"That's okay," Harriet says. Murphy quietly takes Avery's other hand, and Jessica kisses her cheek.

"I'm not done growing," Avery says. "That sounds— stupidly self-aware, I guess, but I'm not. And you're kinda my support system now."

"We want to be," Theresa says.

"You're our family as long as you want to be," Penelope tells her. Lupe smiles at her when Avery glances at her.

"I want to be." Avery squeezes Bunny's hand, and Bunny pulls her in to an embrace. She kisses her again, and her sharp canine teeth press into her lip, only briefly, before she pulls away. The fire keeps burning, sending up plumes of grotesque smoke, but Avery's happier than she's been for the first time in months, surrounded by her coven.

The Fever of Indifference

The ship has false days and real nights. The lights are on during the "daytime," meant to simulate sunlight, because the bodies and brains of the crewmembers need that sort of structure in their lives to function. The daylight and sunshine aren't real; they fill the hallways and the chamber rooms and the bridge with light, but it never feels authentic. It never feels like it did back home. Sometimes, it's better. Sometimes, that lack of natural light and vitamin D makes it so, *so* much worse.

Ezra's taken to walking the halls at night. Well, "night." He's the captain; he can do whatever he wants. The night crew's on the bridge, there's a couple of people eating in the mess hall, and everybody else is asleep. It's a good, quiet time to process whatever's happened that day, that week, that month, his whole *life;* it all just comes spilling out. It hasn't been an easy life, but it's been his, and he wouldn't trade it for anyone else's. Not now, not when he has his own ship and the family that is his crew and a purpose in life, which he had never had before.

Space is lonely, but people make it better. Ezra really believes that.

Ezra takes the long route around the ship, watching the stars flick by through the huge windows. A lot of the walls are made of the thickest windows Ezra's ever seen in his life, but it does make the place feel less like a prison. Everybody feels less trapped when they can see the vast expanse of space constantly.

He passes a couple of people playing chess, one of the players drowsy, yawning as he moves a pawn. They're both on the security team. He knows their names (Audrey and Joshua) because he knows everybody's names on his ship. He knows who is assigned to which rooms. He knows what everybody's title is. He's been inviting people to meals with him so he can get to know them better, beyond their jobs and their room assignments and their names on the rosters. He wants to know their lives, their families, their stories: why they're here, why keeps them here, what they want out of this.

Ezra knows them all like he knows himself. They're an extension of himself. He loves them all like he loves his ship.

When Ezra comes to a window with a person standing at it, he's not surprised. Other people like to walk around at night, too. The sky is beautiful. Everything is beautiful out here.

"Hey," Ezra says. He stuffs his hands in his pockets and goes to stand beside Xavier. Xavier doesn't even turn his head to look at him. He's Ezra's second-in-command, his chief officer, his first mate. They know absolutely everything about each other; they've been on this ship for four years now. Ezra stares out at the sky with him. "What're you looking at?"

"All of it," Xavier tells him. Ezra nods, watching the stars. "Do you ever think about it?"

"What, space?" Ezra asks. "It's our job."

"No," Xavier says. "No, not space. The— Well, in a way, yes, space. The vastness of it, I mean. The unending— all of it. It never ends."

"It ends when we do," Ezra tells him. "That's what I tell myself."

"I can't handle that," Xavier says. He looks down, where the floor meets the window, seamless. "I can't stop thinking about it."

"Space?"

"Dying," Xavier says. "About dying."

Ezra's palms break into a cold sweat. He feels tension pull at his shoulders, yanking along his spine. He tries not to look at Xavier and fails, glancing at him. "You can't stop thinking about dying? Is something wrong?"

Xavier shakes his head. "Nothing's *wrong*. I just— The more I think about it, the more engulfed I become in the concept. We have only one life. We don't get any do-overs."

"No, but that's what makes life so special," Ezra says. "Every day— That's the only chance we get at that day. So, you have to make the most of it."

"I know that," Xavier tells him. "I know that logically. I do. But it doesn't stop me from thinking about dying." Xavier turns his head, and Ezra realizes he never looked away. The two of them stare at each other. "There's no coming back, when I die. When you die. We're just gone. And we won't even *know* that we're gone, we'll just be… nothing. Just nothing." Xavier looks back out at the stars. "I don't know what to do with that."

"I don't think anybody does," Ezra says. "Really."

"That's not comforting," Xavier says. "I wish someone knew. I wish *I* knew. I can't stop thinking about how when you die—" Xavier shuts his eyes, shakes his head. He swallows and starts over. "You're just gone. Your energy is just gone." Xavier opens his eyes, and they're glassy. Ezra's heart starts pounding. "How can you just be gone?"

"I'm still here."

"Not forever." Xavier turns, and Ezra realizes where they're standing. They're near the door hatch, the emergency exit to the ejection pod. Ezra can't take his eyes off of the handle set into the wall, once he sees it.

"What're you doing out here?" Ezra asks.

"Just looking," Xavier tells him, "and thinking."

"About dying?" Ezra pushes. They're both looking at the handle now. Ezra wants to vomit. Xavier doesn't move.

"I don't want to die," Xavier says. "But I can't stop thinking about it."

"Your energy can't be gone, either, man," Ezra rushes to tell him. "We don't have that much time left here. If you're gonna die at the end anyways, you may as well get as many days out of it as you can."

Xavier shrugs.

"No, really," Ezra says, before Xavier can say anything at all. "You think you're freaking out? Man, think about how I feel finding you out by the ejection pod, telling me you can't stop thinking about dying."

"I wouldn't do it," Xavier tells him. Ezra takes his hand out of his pocket and slips it into Xavier's hand.

"Wouldn't you?" Ezra asks. Xavier shakes his head.

"Would you go with me?" Xavier asks without answering. "If I did. Would you?"

Ezra considers it. Genuinely, he thinks about his answer to that question. He loves Xavier more than anyone else on the ship— More than anyone else in his life, really. But he thinks about it, too. The dying. The unending nothingness. He's not ready for it. He has so much left to do. If nearly dying more than once on this ship has taught him anything, it's that every second has value. It's that he can't waste any more time.

"No," Ezra says. "No, I wouldn't die for you. I'd live for you."

Xavier makes a small snorting sound, a little scoff. "That's stupid."

"It's not," Ezra says. "It isn't."

Xavier squeezes his hand.

"You still have so much left to do." Ezra turns Xavier away from the window, away from the ejection pod, away from his own thoughts. "Don't look out there. Don't think about that."

"I can't stop," Xavier whispers. His eyes seem far away; his attention isn't all there in the hall with them. When he blinks, one tear rolls down his face. "It's consuming me."

Ezra pulls Xavier over to the opposite wall and sits them both down on the ground. He pulls Xavier's head against his shoulder, and Xavier goes, nearly limp, letting himself be moved. He exhales shakily. Ezra tucks Xavier's head under his chin and strokes his back. He's not a human, of course, he's an alien, but Ezra is so used to him, it doesn't matter. Xavier has black eyes, Xavier has thick dark-red scales instead of skin, Xavier has a spear stitched in where one arm is supposed to be. It doesn't matter. Xavier likes wearing patterned shirts, Xavier keeps calm in a crisis, Xavier can still hold on with his flesh hand. It's not your species that makes you human. It's your humanity.

"I want to take a break," Xavier says. "A long break."

"A vacation?"

"From life."

"Ah," Ezra says. "That's sleeping."

Xavier laughs. "Sleeping. You *love* sleeping."

"Who *doesn't* love sleeping?" Ezra tells him. "Come on, man. Sleeping's the best. There's so many good things we can do in our lives. Sleep, eat, fuck, dance—"

"Come on," Xavier says, grinning. Ezra buries his face in Xavier's hair.

"*You* come on," Ezra says. "Don't freak me out like this. We still have so much left to do together."

"You're so weird," Xavier tells him. Ezra snorts.

"What, *I'm* so weird?" Ezra asks. "You've got goddamn lizard scales instead of skin."

"Why would I want skin when it's so penetrable?" Xavier asks. "You're so soft. It's a wonder you're not constantly in danger. Well—"

"Yeah, *well*, I am," Ezra says, "it's just because I'm me."

"Humans." Xavier twists around to look up at him. *"You, specifically."*

"Well, don't say it like that," Ezra scolds him. "Say it like... humans! *Yes!* We *love* humans!"

"We'll see," Xavier says. "Humans. You don't have that much time."

"Stop thinking about that," Ezra tells him, voice soft. "Don't waste any of it. That's it. You're already here, you have to die someday, it's inevitable. Just don't waste any of the time you're actually here."

"Fine," Xavier agrees. "But I'm gonna have at least eight more crises this week alone over this, I hope you know that."

"You wouldn't be you if you didn't." Ezra looks out the windowed wall at space as it flies by. Life is strange. "Life is strange."

"Yes," Xavier says. "Yes, it is."

His right hand is a harpoon. His body is a weapon. He's dangerous. He's a threat. He's living. He's alive. He's soft, right now, and tender.

"Thanks," Xavier whispers. Ezra shakes his head.

"Don't mention it," Ezra tells him. He won't; he doesn't.

THE MOST DANGEROUS ANIMAL
OF THEM ALL

Diego has always been very into true crime, ever since he was a teenager. He's researched all the big cases, he has his favorite stories, he's pretty sure he can figure out who the Zodiac Killer really is if he could just connect the dots. He went to school to study forensics, and he got a job in a DNA unit analyzing forensic evidence. He watches all the documentaries. He reads all the books. It's his *thing*.

He never really thought it would affect him personally. He kind of assumed, you know, if he talked and thought about it a lot, the odds would be really low that anything would actually happen to *him*. He never expected anything to happen.

Now, though.

Now, Diego is staring at the DNA results found at a crime scene. Not just any crime scene, either; it's a murder scene, that's the latest in a string of murders, all apparently from one serial killer that just seems impossible to catch. Brutal killings, of evidently random victims, and Diego has been trying to piece together who it could possibly be as they keep bringing his office DNA evidence and fibers and fingerprints.

Diego is staring at the information that's been delivered in the envelope that lays in front of him. He doesn't want to understand it, let alone believe it.

It matches Elliott's file.

"Fuck," Diego whispers.

"What was that?" Nellie asks. Diego slams the folder shut.

"Nothing," he says. "Sorry, I just— banged my elbow."

"Alright," Nellie says, curling back over her work. Diego opens the folder back up on his desk and flips through the pages. Elliott was fingerprinted once when he was a child as part of an initiative to build a database should children go missing; he'd never been arrested or had any other reason to have his DNA in any database.

Elliott, who makes his own passionflower tea. Elliott, who grows his own vegetables in his own garden to cook with. Elliott, who tears up reading romance novels late at night. Elliott, who Diego has been hopelessly in love with for five years.

This can't be real, Diego thinks. There's no reason Elliott's DNA would be at this crime scene, so there has to be *another* reason. Maybe he knew the victim somehow, or maybe he sold them a knitted scarf at one of those craft fairs he's always tabling at. Something like that. *Anything* that— that disproves Elliott being there for any other reason.

Diego shuts the folder again, slips it back into its envelope, stuffs it into his briefcase, and stands, chair screeching backwards across the floor. Nellie barely glances at him.

"I'm cutting out early," Diego says. Nellie keeps working.

"See you tomorrow," Nellie replies. Diego snaps his briefcase shut and rushes out to his car, fumbling with the keys as he tries to get them in the lock.

"Shit, shit, *shit,*" he whispers, shoving his house key into the door. He stops, stares at it. Then, he rolls his shoulders, shuts his eyes, and takes a long, deep breath.

"It's just a weird coincidence," he tells himself, voice firm and unwavering. "I'll ask Elliott about it and he'll explain it and I'll feel stupid. It's fine." He opens his eyes, pulls the key out of the lock, and finally finds the car key to unlock the door. "It's *fine.*"

The drive home is usually only about twenty minutes, but today it alternatively feels like twenty seconds or two hours. He tries to take deep breaths all the way home. He turns the radio on, but it's too much noise for his brain to process along with the frantic humming of his own thoughts, and so he turns it back off.

He pulls into their driveway and stares up at their house for a long, long moment. They've lived together in this house for three years. When did Elliott—

"Stop," Diego says, out loud. "That's stupid. He didn't do anything."

His hands are still shaking when he pulls the key out of the ignition and drags himself up to the front door. He unlocks the door and makes his way inside. There's no sign of Elliott, but their two Newfoundland dogs, Amy and Jo, come bounding out to slam into his legs. He scratches their heads as he heads into their kitchen, popping open his briefcase and pulling out the envelope again. He looks at it for a while before pulling the folder out once more, flipping it open to read the case details.

"Hey," Elliott calls, from deep inside the house. Diego slams the folder shut. "Diego? That you?"

"Yeah," Diego calls back. His voice cracks a little. There's a moment of silence before Diego hears footsteps heading down the stairs and towards the kitchen. Elliott appears in the entryway within minutes.

"Something wrong?" Elliott asks. "Your voice sounded a little off." Elliott looks him over, then frowns. "Jesus, you look pale. Did something happen at work? You okay?"

Diego looks at him for a while. Then, he opens the folder back up, glancing down at the names of the victims. "Do you know Brianna Parsons and Shaun Stanford?"

Elliott doesn't say anything. After one long, horrible, moment, Diego looks up at him, but Elliott's looking at the folder on the table in front of him.

"What's that?" Elliott asks.

"Eli," Diego says, voice cracking again. Elliott's eyes dart up to his face. "Do you know them?"

Elliott scans Diego's face, searching for something. Diego doesn't know what he's looking for, but he lets him seek it for as long as he wants.

"I do," Elliott says. He crosses the room, and the air feels thick. The moment seems almost impenetrable. There's energy crackling between them. Diego's afraid of it. He looks down at the folder. "What's this?"

"Case file," Diego answers. Elliott leans over him, lifts the page about the case to look at the DNA results on the next piece of paper. He reads it for a few moments.

"Ahh," Elliott says. He slides the case papers out of the way to look at the fingerprint analysis. "It matched me."

"Did you sell them a scarf?" Diego asks. He feels stupid as soon as he asks it. Elliott, to his credit, doesn't even look at him, doesn't give him an exasperated look or shout at him for even kind of believing he could be involved.

"No," Elliott says. Diego's heart rate picks up a little bit. His hands feel tingly and cold.

"How did you know them?" Diego asks. Elliott keeps looking at the fingerprints on the paper, *his* fingerprints, standing over Diego at the kitchen table. Diego's abruptly glad he sat down before this started, because he doesn't think his legs would've been holding him up anymore.

Eventually, Elliott puts the papers back in order and shuts the folder. He sits down in the chair next to Diego, the chair he always sits in to eat, and looks at Diego across the table.

"Shaun Stanford was scamming old women out of their money over the phone," Elliott says. Diego shuts his eyes and puts his face in his hands. "Brianna Parsons was his girlfriend. She helped him do it."

"What did you do?" Diego asks, eyes still closed.

"I gave them what they deserved," Elliott says. Diego shoves his chair back and stands, pacing to the far wall of the kitchen and then back to the table, faster than he's ever moved before.

"What the *fuck* did you *do, Eli?"* Diego demands. Elliott stares up at him.

"I told you," Elliott says. "They were scamming old ladies. They had to die."

"They had to— *What the fuck do you mean,* 'they had to die'?" Diego asks. "What the *fuck?* They were— What, they were scamming old ladies? How the hell does that equal fucking death? What the *fuck?"*

"The old ladies just wanted company, those two were taking advantage of them," Elliott explains, before he says, "You're freaking out."

"Of *course* I'm freaking out," Diego exclaims. "Why the *fuck* wouldn't I be? You fucking *killed* two people because they were pulling a phone scam!"

Elliott stares up at him, then says, "Not exactly."

Diego runs his fingers up into his hair, holds onto it. It's the only thing his hands can think to do. "What does that mean?"

"I haven't exactly killed two people," Elliott clarifies. Diego's brain is racing.

"You didn't do it alone?" Diego asks, and he's mad at himself that his first response is jealousy. *Elliott has a partner he kills people with?* He didn't even think to ask Diego about it? He has someone who knows about this more secret part of himself, and that person isn't Diego? That kind of hurts.

Then, Diego reminds himself that he's talking about fucking *murder* here, and shakes off the feeling.

"No, I did it alone," Elliott says, and Diego feels a twisted sort of relief at that. "I just didn't kill *only* two people."

Diego stares at him. He remembers, then— This case is the most recent in a string of murders that the cops are pretty sure are all from one person. A serial killer, terrorizing the city.

The serial killer who's sitting right in front of him, who still has a little bit of blue paint of his hands, because he was probably touching up the paint in the bathroom like Diego had asked him to do last weekend.

"Why?" Diego asks, because it's the only thing he can think to ask, in that moment. "Why— *Why* did you do it? Why are you doing this?"

"They all deserve it," Elliott says. "Stacey Northrop hit her kids, Toby Phillips was cheating on his wife, Irma Walters drowned birds in her birdbath, Lloyd Lawson was stealing from the corner store, Denise Foster cut you off in traffic—"

"Wha— Wait, hold the fuck up," Diego interrupts, head spinning. "First— Wait, Denise Foster cut me off in traffic?"

"Yeah, a couple of months ago," Elliott says.

"So you killed her?"

"It wasn't the *fact* that she cut you off," Elliott says. "It was the *way* she did it. She was so smug about it. She did it all the time, you know."

"I don't— Jesus Christ," Diego says, rubbing at his face. He presses the heels of his hands against his closed eyes until he sees stars. "How many people have you killed?"

There's silence.

"*Elliott,*" Diego insists.

"I'm counting, hold on," Elliott says, and Diego storms back to the far wall, starting his pacing all over again.

"You shouldn't have to *count,* holy shit, you're going to jail," Diego says. He sits down on the floor, right where he is, on the cold kitchen linoleum, and presses his forehead to his knees. "Jesus *fuck!* You're going to go to jail!"

"I haven't been caught yet," Elliott says. When Diego looks up at him, he's standing.

"We matched your DNA!" Diego exclaims. "We matched your DNA and your fingerprints at the crime scene. It's you. They have your *fingerprints.*"

"No," Elliott says. "No, *you* have my fingerprints."

Diego stares up at him.

"Think about it," Elliott says. "Does anybody else have this information?"

"I don't know!" Diego says. His voice is getting dangerously high and manic. "I don't fucking— Whoever sent me this file, I guess? Whoever did the fingerprint matches? I just do the DNA matches. Pete Nicholson does the fingerpri—" Diego stops abruptly, looks up, points at Elliott. "Do *not* kill Pete Nicholson, I *swear to God.*"

"I'll find out what he knows," Elliott says, and Diego's more than aware that that is *not* an agreement, but there's so

347

much going on that he can't focus for too long on worrying about Pete Nicholson. "But, seriously, Diego, think about it. You're the only one who has the information. You. That's it. You have the papers. You have the evidence. What do *you* want to do about it?"

Diego stares up at him. Elliott crosses the room to him, sits down next to him with his legs folded, and starts rubbing his back. Diego rests his cheek on his knees and watches him.

"Why?" Diego asks, softly.

"Why what?" Elliott replies.

"Why do you do it?" Diego clarifies. Elliott keeps rubbing his back.

"I told you, they deserve it," Elliott says. "Somebody has to do it."

"You're fucking insane," Diego states. Elliott just keeps on rubbing his back. "How many people have you killed? You didn't answer me."

"I think eleven, so far," Elliott says. Diego turns his face into his knees again. "I was thinking about maybe going after Herbie Roscoe next, he's been getting really aggressive with the cashiers at that fast food place near the corner of Elm and Tower, what's that place—"

"Holy shit, you really are insane," Diego interrupts him. "I can't believe this. I kept telling myself the whole way here, I kept saying, 'Don't overreact, because he'll have a rational explanation for everything,' but your fucking *rational explanation* is that people fucking— They cut me off in traffic or they're mean to waitresses or they scam old ladies so you fucking chop their heads off? How the *fuck* does that make any sense?"

"I think you're freaking out," Elliott says. Diego laughs, hysterical.

"Oh, do you?" Diego asks. "Do you think I'm freaking out? I can't possibly imagine why the *fuck* I'd be freaking out right now."

Elliott stops rubbing his back and scoots around to sit in front of him. "Can you take a deep breath for me?"

"Oh, fucking—"

"Diego," Elliott says, firmly. Diego lifts his head to look at him. "Take a deep breath. Calm down."

Diego, against his better judgment, takes a deep breath, because he *is* getting a little light-headed. Elliott takes deep breaths with him, and Diego matches his pace, matches the depth. The two of them just sit there on the floor, evening out Diego's breathing, for a couple of minutes. At the end of it, Diego's heart is still racing, but he feels calmer. There's a coolness leaking around the edges of his thoughts as he tries to process everything.

"I don't have a good answer for you," Elliott says, after a little while. Diego just watches him. "I don't. I just do this. It feels like the right thing to do."

Diego stares at him. Then, he asks the question that's been tugging at him for a little while now: "Why didn't you tell me?"

Elliott frowns at him. His eyebrows always pull together when he frowns, and he gets a little crease between his eyes. It's cute. "What?"

"The police said the guy's— I mean, that *you*," Diego corrects. "The police said you've been killing for a few months now. At least since last year, right?"

"Yeah," Elliott says. "The first one was Irving Massey, and that was last June."

"So, a little over a year ago," Diego says. "Why didn't you tell me?"

"That I was killing people?" Elliott asks. Diego nods. "Uhh. I feel like that's self-explanatory, to be totally honest with you—"

"But it's me," Diego says, and isn't that just the end-all be-all crux of the thing. Elliott is a serial killer and possibly completely off his *nut,* but he's still Diego's partner and has been for years, and he's been keeping such a huge secret, and that's sort of what hurts the most, right now. "I tell you everything."

"You telling me everything means telling me when you stole a yogurt at work or when you have gossip about the neighbors," Elliott says. Diego just keeps looking at him, because they both know that's not what he meant. Eventually, Elliott sighs. "Yeah, I know. I'm sorry. I just didn't know how to tell you. They don't exactly have cards for this at the store."

Diego huffs a laugh and scrubs at his face with his hands again. He lets his legs fall so his knees aren't pressed against his chest, spreading them out so Elliott is situated between them. Elliott wraps one hand around Diego's ankle and squeezes. Diego looks him over, all six-foot-two of his gangly body folded into the space between Diego's legs. His black hair is pulled back from his face right now in a headband, and his dark eyes are warm and familiar. Diego sighs.

"I'm going to destroy the folder," Diego says. Elliott exhales sharply. "And I'll find out what Pete knows, leave him alone. I'll fix that. I'll just tell him I brought something home to work on and you accidentally touched it."

"That's unprofessional," Elliott says. Diego smiles, despite himself.

"It's better than you getting arrested, isn't it?" Diego asks, and Elliott shrugs, grinning back at him. "Jesus *Christ.* What the fuck is wrong with us?"

"Somebody has to do it," Elliott repeats. "Did you want to help me with it?"

Diego actually considers it for a second, but then he thinks about actually chopping somebody's head off and his stomach turns. "No, thank you."

"You can be the business end of things," Elliott says. "Making sure I don't get caught."

"God, this just goes against— against *everything* they've ever told us," Diego says. Elliott stands up, holds out his hand. Diego takes it and lets Elliott haul him to his feet.

"What, they *told* you not to be an accomplice?" Elliott asks. Diego huffs a laugh.

"Jesus fuck, I'm an accomplice now," Diego says. Elliott kisses him on the forehead.

"Couldn't ask for a better partner," Elliott says, then continues, "in *crime.*"

Diego laughs, says, "I hate you." Elliott pulls him in, hugs him, kisses his forehead again.

"No, you don't," Elliott says.

———

The phone rings while Diego is making dinner. Elliott is out late, doing whatever he's doing, so Diego wipes his hands off on a dish towel and answers the phone himself.

"Hello?" he asks, wedging the phone in between his head and his shoulder, holding it there while he returns to the stove. The cord just barely reaches to allow him to stand there and keep stirring his sauce.

"Hey, it's me," Elliott says on the other end. "I just had a quick question for you."

"Shoot," Diego says. He just added the peas and mushrooms to the sauce, and he's waiting for them to be cooked well enough to add the smoked salmon.

"These people have a shitty window," Elliott explains. Diego can hear him shuffling, probably dragging something. "It started to slide shut while I was in here when *someone* slammed into the wall." It sounds like Elliott is scolding someone, but nobody responds. "So, I grabbed it to stop it from slamming, and now it has my fingerprints on it. How do I get them all the way off?"

"First of all, that was stupid," Diego says, stirring his sauce.

"Save the lecture for tonight," Elliott tells him. Diego can hear the smile in his voice. "What do I do right *now?*"

"Honestly, the best thing to do would be to put your gloves back on and find some sort of cleaning solution," Diego says. "Once you clean it, smash it."

There's a beat of silence. "Smash it?"

"Yeah," Diego says. "Then it'll be in pieces and if anything's left behind, it'll be hard to put it back together. If they do— Well, it'll come to me anyways, right?"

"Yeah, I stayed in your district this time," Elliott says.

"Then just do that," Diego tells him. "Clean it, then smash it. And please wear your gloves for the rest of the night."

"Got it," Elliott says. "Love you."

"Love you, too," Diego says. "I'm almost done making dinner, so finish up."

"Can do," Elliott says. "Bye."

"Bye," Diego echoes, and hangs up. He tosses the smoked salmon into the pot and keeps stirring. He finishes the dish, plates it, and he's part of the way through his own plate when he hears the front door open and close.

"I need some help," Elliott calls. Diego sighs. He takes a sip of his wine and stands, going to the entryway to find Elliott standing on the mat. He's got blood splattered across his entire front, from shoes to face. He grins. "Help?"

"Jesus," Diego says. It somehow never stops being surprising, seeing Elliott like this. "Who was it tonight, again?"

"Terry and Linda Smalls," Elliott tells him, as Diego digs a paper bag out of the hall closet. "They're the ones who I saw kick—"

"—kick their dog," Diego finishes. "Yeah, I remember."

"They deserved it," Elliott asserts. Diego peels his jacket off for him and shoves it in the paper bag. "Terry was the one who tripped into the wall. It was embarrassing, really." He ducks down to let Diego tug his shirt off over his head. "I cut his hands off and threw them in a lake on the way back."

"You threw his hands in the Wareborough Lake?" Diego asks. Elliott shakes his head.

"No, the Carcook Reservoir," Elliott says. "I made a loop so it wouldn't be too close to home."

"Thank you."

"You're welcome." Elliott steps out of his shoes and pants, and Diego shoves them in the bag. Once he's stripped down to nothing, Diego points up the stairs.

"Go shower," Diego orders, and Elliott goes. "Don't drip anywhere!"

"It's mostly dry!" Elliott calls back down the stairs. Diego ties the paper bag shut and takes it down to the basement, where it's eaten by the incinerator. Diego watches the clothes and bag turn to ash, then he shuts the door on the thing and goes back upstairs to the bathroom. He sits on the closed toilet seat while Elliott scrubs himself down.

"I brought you something," Elliott says.

"Please don't be a head," Diego jokes. It's only kind of a joke, because Elliott did bring a head back with him once, and Diego had come home to find the head sitting on the coffee table in the living room.

"It's not a head this time," Elliott calls back. "It's in my wallet."

Diego picks Elliott's wallet up off the counter next to the sink and opens it, digging through the dollar bills and cards and photos until he finds a folded-up card. Curious, he pulls it out and unfolds it. He laughs when he reads the front.

"'I'd kill to be with you,'" he reads out loud. "Jesus Christ. Where did you find this?"

"That dollar store down the street," Elliott tells him. He sticks his head out of the shower, and his face is streaked with pink. His dark hair drips onto the floor, but that's clean already, at least. "Turns out they *do* have cards for this at the store."

"You're such an ass," Diego says. Elliott laughs, ducking back into the shower. "Hurry up, your pasta's getting cold."

"Can do," Elliott calls to him. Diego smoothes out the card in his hands and sets it on the counter, leaning against the mirror. "I'd kill for you!"

"Shut the fuck up," Diego shouts back. He leans his chin in his hand and looks at the card on the counter for a while before he sighs and grabs the bleach from under the sink to scrub the shower tiles with.

THEN THERE'S A PAIR OF US!

Sadie has a good sense of humor. She's a detective, an investigator, and she calls herself a *private eye,* despite the fact that she's blind as a bat. Always has been, since she was about seven, when she fell from a fire escape. Gave herself a nasty knock to the head, but she's alright now. She can't see, but she's been blind for nearly thirty years now, and she's adapted just fine to it all.

Her phone rings in her office. She hears Ruthie pick it up. Ruthie is the best secretary she's ever had, because she doesn't patronize her. She's warm and kind and sometimes brings leftovers from her family dinners for Sadie to take home with her. Sadie loves her.

"Hello?" Ruthie asks. Sadie half-listens as she toys with a knick-knack from her desk. It has random sharp edges; it was given to her as a gift. She and Ruthie have made a game out of

Sadie guessing what it is and Ruthie telling her if she's getting warmer or colder. She hasn't quite guessed it yet.

"Yes, she's here, she stays all night on Saturdays," Ruthie says into the phone. "Would you like to speak with her?" Silence as Ruthie listens. Then, "Alright, then. Would you like to leave a message?" Another beat of silence. "Hello? Would you like— Oh, gosh." Ruthie hangs up.

"Who was that?" Sadie calls from her office. She hears Ruthie stand up and come to stand in her doorway.

"Someone who asked if you were still in," Ruthie tells her. "Told them you'd be here all night, seeing as it's a Saturday."

"And they just hung up?" Sadie asks. She kicks her feet up onto her desk, toying with the paperweight. "That's odd. Maybe they're planning on stopping by."

"Maybe," Ruthie says, but she sounds uncertain. Sadie cocks her head in her direction.

"What is it?" Sadie asks. Ruthie's gut instincts are usually pretty good, so Sadie always wants to hear about them.

"He just sounded... funny," Ruthie tells her. "Not in a ha-ha way, in an odd way. Too intense."

"I'll keep an ear out," Sadie says. Ruthie laughs softly. "Is it a globe?"

"You've guessed that before," Ruthie says. "Colder. It's not a globe."

"Damn." Sadie sets the knick-knack down and drops her feet to the floor. "Getting ready to head out?"

"Just about got my things together," Ruthie tells her. There's a rustle, and then something is dropped onto Sadie's desk. "I brought you two sandwiches. A Friday burger and an apple-and-cheese sandwich. I know you got hungry last week."

"Ruthie, you're a goddess," Sadie says. "Tell Otis and Gregory I said hello."

"Gregory can't even speak yet," Ruthie replies, but she always says that. She tells Gregory hello anyways, every time. "I'll see you on Monday?"

"Absolutely," Sadie agrees. She hears Ruthie's heels click across the floor, and then Ruthie kisses her on the top of the head. "You're too good to me."

"I know," Ruthie says. She smoothes Sadie's hair down, pinches her cheek, and leaves. Sadie hears her gathering up her things before she leaves through the front door of their office. Sadie sits back in her chair again once she's gone, kicking her feet back up onto her desk and picking up the paperweight again. Ruthie's probably messing with her and it *is* just a globe, because it *feels* like a globe, and if it walks like a duck and talks like a duck—

The front door opens and shuts again.

"Forget something, Ruthie?" Sadie calls out, tossing the knick-knack between her hands. No answer. She puts her feet on the ground. "Gee, sorry, is someone looking for me?" Still no answer. She sets the paperweight down. "Hello? Someone there?"

Still nothing. Sadie leans back; it was probably the office next door. Sometimes she mixes up the sounds. It *had* sounded like theirs, but nobody's saying anything. Sadie slides her fingers along her desktop until she finds the bag with the sandwiches in it, and she digs one out. She takes a bite of one, just for the spontaneity of it: it's the Friday burger.

"Oh, hell yes," Sadie murmurs to herself. Ruthie's tuna somehow tastes better than anyone else's that Sadie's ever had. As she goes for a second bite, she hears a tiny *creak*. The sandwich stops halfway to her mouth.

"Hello?" Sadie asks again. "Is somebody in here?" Nothing. Sadie sighs and puts the sandwich back down in the bag. "If someone's in here, please don't steal anything from me. I'm blind, not stupid." Sadie slowly opens her desk drawer, withdrawing her pistol. "You should probably leave if you don't want to do business. I'm a pretty good shot."

Another creak. Sadie turns her head slightly, trying to listen better. She cocks her pistol. "Look, buddy, you don't want to be here right now. Tell me what you want and get out."

"What do *you* want, Sadie Appleton?" a man's voice asks, and Sadie's head whips around towards the corner of the room.

"I want you to tell me what you want and get out," Sadie says. She's been a private eye for a long time; her voice doesn't waver when she makes orders. "I thought I made that pretty clear the first time."

There's a creak. This one is on the opposite side of the room. Sadie sighs.

"We heard you'd be here all night," the same man's voice says. "We have a case for you."

"What case is that?" Sadie asks.

"Missing private eye," the man tells her. There's another creak. Sadie doesn't roll her eyes, but she wants to.

"That's a terrible line," Sadie says. "So, what'd I do? Did your wife leave you? Did you get fired? Whatever it was, it's not *my* fault just because I caught you. You shouldn't have been doing whatever it was in the first place, I guarantee it."

"That's not why I'm here," the man says. He sounds like he's near the doorway now.

"Then why are you here?" Sadie asks.

"Because you are," the man tells her. There's another creak that makes him sound like he's left the room, and Sadie fires his pistol in the direction of the doorway. She doesn't hear it hit anything; her ears are ringing as she tries to listen for another footstep. She darts under her desk with the bullets from her drawer to reload her pistol and shoves her extra bullets into her pockets. She exhales slowly, quietly. She can't hear anything, but she also can't shake the feeling that she's being hunted.

"I'm a great shot," Sadie calls out. "You'd better be careful."

"Of course you are," the man says, nearly right in front of her, and Sadie fires again. She hears the bullet enter the wall, but there's no groan or impact through flesh. He's already gone. He's too quiet, too light on his feet. He knows she can't see and he's using it. The thought makes her heart skip a beat.

"Wherever you are, you'd better get out," Sadie says. "I'm calling the police!"

Sadie hears the man laugh from the next room. "With what phone?"

Sadie scrambles up, grabs her telephone off the cradle, and holds the receiver to her ear. The line is dead. She slams it back into the cradle and retreats into the corner of her room, so she has her back covered. She holds her pistol steady and listens. Still nothing. Heart pounding, she slides her hand flat along the wall, until she reaches the window latch. She starts to unlock the window.

"I wouldn't do that if I were you," the man's voice says. Sadie's hands both grip onto her gun and she levels it in the direction of his voice.

"Get over here and fight me like a man," Sadie orders him. He laughs again.

"Why bother?" he asks. "This is so much more fun."

Sadie fires a shot in his direction. Again, no impact. Sadie listens for him, but it doesn't sound like he's moving.

"What are you doing?" she asks. He doesn't answer. He's clever, and strange, and— likely the man who was on the phone before. *Damn it.* She fires again, same direction, and still nothing. She hears clomping on the steps outside the office, as if someone is running up the stairs, and she turns in the direction of the man's voice, making sure her eyes are making contact where his eyes should be. She hopes it unnerves him.

"Someone's coming," she tells him. No answer. "You'd better get out."

The front door of the office slams open, and Ruthie shouts, "Sadie, what's happening?"

"There's someone in here with me," Sadie calls out. She hears Ruthie drop her bag near the door and come sprinting into her office.

"I don't see anyone," Ruthie says. She sounds frantic, frightened. "I heard the gunshots downstairs, I had to come back up and check on you. Is he hiding somewhere?"

"I don't know," Sadie says. They only have one door in and out of the place, and all the windows are closed. Sadie's heart is pounding. "I really don't know. You don't see anyone?"

"Let me look," Ruthie tells her. Sadie holds out a hand, and Ruthie comes over and takes it, lightly. Sadie slips the pistol into her fingers. Ruthie leaves with it; Sadie can hear her looking around the office.

"There's nobody up here," Ruthie calls back. She comes back into the entryway. "There's nobody in here. Are you sure he didn't go out the door? Or a window?"

"I don't know," Sadie says. She *is* sure, and he didn't. He's still here, or he wasn't here, or— Sadie can't *think,* she can't figure it out. Her pulse is roaring in her ears. "I don't know, I'm sorry."

"It's okay," Ruthie tells her. She puts the gun back into Sadie's hand. "Why don't you come home with me? Stay over tonight. You know Gregory loves to see you."

Sadie's still catching her breath, but she nods. "Okay. Yeah, okay."

"Okay," Ruthie says. "Wanna put the gun back in your desk?"

Sadie doesn't want to, but she does anyways, unloading it and sliding it back into the drawer. She lets Ruthie help her pack up her things and lead her out of the office, shutting the door behind them and locking it. As they leave, a chill slides down Sadie's spine.

"Come back tomorrow and we'll do it all again," the man's voice whispers in her ear, and Sadie turns without thinking and punches her fist into the wall.

"Sadie, what the hell?" Ruthie shouts. She still sounds frightened. "Why— Why did you do that?"

"He was just right there," Sadie tells her. "I just— I heard him, he was right behind me—"

"There's nobody there," Ruthie says. Sadie cradles her fist in her other hand; she can feel the bruises forming already. The chill slithers away, leaving her feeling empty. She twists her head around towards Ruthie, trying to listen, but there's nothing to be heard. There's only silence. "There's nobody there."

ROUX-GA-ROUX

Rowan is not a man, but everybody thinks she is, because she's the king's manservant. She understands why people thinks she's a man. It's because she told everyone that she's a man when she first came to the castle town of Valcester. When she arrived, nobody was looking for wives or handmaidens or anything like that, but the king was seeking new manservants. She cut her hair, got a set of men's clothes, and approached the then-crown prince, George, about being taken on as his manservant.

So, Rowan has been King George's manservant since he was the crown prince. She was with him through his father's death, through his coronation, and now, through the first few months of his rule.

She also loves him.

She *loves* George, and she's a liar, so she's not allowed to love him. She lies to him every day, because he believes she's a man, and she doesn't know how to tell him that she isn't. It's such a strange lie, but it was all she could think of at the time, and now she's in too deep to get out.

Rowan can't figure out what to do *about* loving George, though. There's a lot of layers to it. One, she's lying to him, obviously. He thinks that she's a man. Rowan's pretty sure he's interested, which might be its *own* problem: if he's interested in men, he wouldn't be interested in her. It's a whole tangled-up mess.

The second problem is that George is the *king*. He's the actual, literal king, and that means any marriage of his would probably be for political reasons. Even if it wasn't, he could marry absolutely anybody he wanted in the whole goddamn world. His manservant is probably at the bottom of that list. Even if he *was* interested, he's probably not interested in marriage. Rowan knows how kings work, she knows the game of it all; he'd probably just want to take her as a lover on the side, if he took her as anything.

The third problem, and easily the most confusing problem, is that George seems to have his *own* secret. He vanishes for a couple of nights every month. Rowan hasn't figured out why he does it, where he goes, or what he's doing, but she knows he's going somewhere, because when she comes to his chambers at night to prepare him for bed, he's always got a bag ready to go. When she returns the next morning to get him up and dressed and ready for the day, his bed isn't slept in and he usually looks exhausted.

Her best guess had been that he had a secret lover somewhere in town, and their arrangement called for him to go to them a couple of nights out of the month, but he never looks happy when he comes back. He just looks tired and sad and drained. It gnaws at her when she sees him like that in the mornings, looking so broken, barely making eye contact with her, staring at the wall. He moves mechanically, hardly speaks, and it's so unlike his usual bombastic, easygoing self that it *aches*.

It's been going on for a couple of years. Rowan didn't know what to do about it at first, so she did nothing. Now, she's pretty much able to predict when it's going to happen. She makes soup and comes prepared with softer words and gentle hands. She wants to stop whatever is hurting him from hurting him. She thinks they would consider themselves friends, at least, and friends don't let each other suffer like this.

Rowan realizes it's another one of those nights when she shows up in George's chambers to bring him food. He hadn't showed up for that night's meal, and she guessed it was because it was another one of his secret days. She's right.

"My king," she says, as a way of greeting, when she inches through the crack in the door with her platter of soup and bread. "How are you feeling?"

"What?" George asks. He's just sitting on the edge of his grand bed, staring at the wall. He turns to look at her once he realizes she's actually there. "Oh. I'm fine. How are you?"

"I'm well, thank you," Rowan tells him. She sets the platter down on the table by the fireplace, lights the logs in the hearth aflame, and then just— stands there. The air in the room is different, like it typically is around this time. "Is something wrong?"

"No," he says, like he always does. Every time, he pretends everything is fine, even when it's clearly not. He smiles at her. "It's just been a long day."

Rowan nods and turns to pour the soup into the bowl and prepare the bread for him. With her back turned, it's easier to say, "You can tell me anything and I would never tell a soul. You know that, right?"

She's met with silence. She finishes arranging the meal, then turns back to him. "Honestly. You're my best— You're my king. Your secrets are safe with me."

George looks at her, not speaking a word. He doesn't seem angry, or confused. He's just staring. Rowan lets him, staring right back. Eventually, he shakes his head, looking away.

"This is not a secret I'm allowed to share," George says. "Even with you."

Rowan wants to ask what that *means,* what he could possibly mean when he says something like *even with you,* but she doesn't. Instead, she takes a couple of steps closer. He looks up at her again.

"Servants are like walls," Rowan says. "We see and hear everything, and never tell." She pauses. "And we keep you safe."

"Do you?" George asks.

"Well, I do," Rowan tells him, and George smiles. He stands.

"Have some soup," he tells her. "I'm not in the mood for it myself."

Rowan glances back at the meal. "But you haven't eaten today."

"Have you?" George asks, and she doesn't answer. "Eat something."

"Only if you do," she says. They stare each other down for a moment before he concedes, taking his armchair beside the fire. He motions to her.

"Come sit," he says, and she briefly thinks he means to sit on his lap, and she feels her face growing warm before she realizes he's motioning to the chair beside him. She takes it, sitting on the very edge, and he hands her half the bread.

"Thank you," she tells him. They eat in silence for a bit. George doesn't speak, and he's usually the first one to break the silence, so Rowan waits. She eats her bread, dunking it in the soup when George pushes the bowl across the platter towards her.

"It's not that I don't want to tell you," George says, eventually. "Because I do. If I was to share this secret with *anyone*, it would be you." He says this so forcefully that Rowan feels a little stunned. She also feels a wave of guilt, that he wants to share his secret while she just keeps lying to him about hers. She can't lose her job, but she can't lose him, either. "But I can't. I just— It's too dangerous."

"Dangerous?" Rowan asks, too surprised for tact. She forgets herself and says, "If it's dangerous, I should be helping you."

"You shouldn't."

"Yes, I should," Rowan says, rising to her feet. "It's my job."

"It's not the job of a manservant to defend a king," George tells her.

"No, it's *my* job," Rowan says. He stares up at her, but she doesn't blink, doesn't look away. Just stands there, staring back. Eventually, George stands, as well. He puts a hand on her shoulder and holds her there, tightly. His palm is huge and hot, and she almost buckles under his touch.

"If you came with me," George says, "you would be in more danger than I would be without you. I can't allow that to happen."

Rowan doesn't know what to say to argue back. She wants to, but he looks so desperate that she can't come up with the words.

"I have to go," George tells her, before she manages to say anything. He lets her go and leaves her standing there by the crackling fire. He hefts his bag over his shoulder and stops beside her. "Don't tell anyone."

"I haven't," she says. "I won't."

"Good," he says. "Don't follow me."

Rowan doesn't answer. He looks her over for a moment. His hand twitches up, then stops before it touches her. She wishes he hadn't stopped, but he did, and he leaves. She stands there in his chambers, with only the fire for company, for a long moment. Then, in a flash of a decision, she douses the fire with water and slips out into the darkened hallway. She can still hear George's footsteps down the hall, and she follows them, creeping along the wall, silent. She knows which stones would shift and which stairs would creak, and nobody knows she's there, including George. She follows him out of the castle in shadows.

He heads to the stables, and she follows him there, careful not to step on any of the loose rustling hay underfoot. He goes to a corner of the stables and opens a trap in the floor. She watches from behind a dividing wall as he kicks out a rope ladder and climbs down into the hole in the stable floors, closing the trap door behind himself. She waits for a bit before going over to investigate the door herself. It's hidden into the floorboards. She finds the little rope that serves as a handle and pulls it up, slowly, to hide its creak.

It's pitch-black inside the room underneath the stables, so she carefully lowers the rope ladder she'd seen George use and climbs down it. She pulls the door down after herself and hauls the rope ladder back up after she touches the ground. She's in complete darkness, but then she hears the sound of a fire striker lighting and a torchlight fills the room.

"What— No," George's voice says, and once Rowan's eyes adjust, she sees him on the other side of the little space, holding a torch, The room is empty, except for a set of chains built into the stone floor. George's face looks terrified. "Why did you come down here?"

"What are you doing?" Rowan asks, barely even processing his question in her confusion. His bag is in the corner, next to the chains. "What— Why?"

"You have to leave," George tells her. Rowan looks down at the chains again.

"No," she says, staring at the metal as the flames flicker, throwing the room into ever-shifting shadows.

"This is an order," George says, but she looks back at him so quickly he frowns.

"I don't care," she tells him. "I'm not going anywhere until you tell me what's happening."

George looks torn, desperate and frightened and angry and maybe happy? His face is confusing, his expression conflicted, and he says, "I can't."

"Then I'm staying," Rowan tells him. She feels bad for trying to force his hand, so, in a split second, she makes a decision. "I have a secret, too."

George's brow furrows. "What? What could you possibly—"

"I do," Rowan interrupts him. "I've always had it. It's... I don't know. I didn't want to lose my job." Rowan stops, looks at George. She has to decide whether or not to say the next part, and she chooses, in this moment: in for a penny, in for a pound. "Or you. I didn't want to lose you if you found out."

"Whatever it is can't be that bad," George tells her. "Tell me tomorrow. Leave, now, before you can't."

"What's that supposed to mean?" Rowan asks. "I'm not going anywhere. I'll tell you my secret if you tell me yours."

George just keeps looking at her, a frown on his round face. "I—" He cuts himself off, stops. "Are you in danger?"

"Probably not," Rowan says. "I mean, if I lose my job, I'll probably end up homeless. But, otherwise, I guess not."

George looks her over. "What could you possibly have done?"

"Swear you'll tell me," Rowan says. "If I tell you my secret, you have to tell me yours. Swear it."

George keeps staring at her. The lights from the flames dance along his face. "Okay."

"Say it," Rowan tells him. She *tells* the King to do something. She shouldn't, but she does, and he doesn't even seem to care.

"I swear," George echoes. Rowan nods, then tugs off her hat and starts untying her doublet. "What are you—"

"Hush," Rowan tells him. She pulls the strings loose and slides the doublet off, then tugs her shirt up and off, as well, revealing her bindings underneath. George stares at her, and this strange underground room is deadly silent for a long, long moment.

"You're a woman," George finally says. "Why did you lie?"

"I needed work," Rowan tells him. "All that was available at the time was being your manservant. And then, after I met you— I didn't want to lose the job."

"Why did you lie to *me?*" George clarifies. Rowan looks away.

"I didn't want to lose you," Rowan tells the wall. "I didn't know what you'd say or do. If you'd be forced to get rid of me. If you'd hate me for it. I wasn't— I didn't mean to trick you or anything. I didn't lie about anything else, just this."

"I don't hate you," George says. "I don't."

"I'm sorry," Rowan says. She can feel her face burning, can feel the back of her eyes and her nose prickling, but she forces herself not to cry. "I'm *so* sorry. I should've told you."

"I can't be mad at you," George tells her. She glances back up at him. "I'm not mad. I get it. I just wish— I thought you'd feel safe enough to tell me. I'm mad that you didn't think you could trust me."

"I didn't know what to do," Rowan says. "You're the king. I don't know why you even bother with me."

George looks at her. "Yes, you do."

Rowan does. "Yes, I do." She's always known. She just has never known what to do about it. She looks away again. "But you— I mean. I'm not a man."

"That doesn't matter to me," George says. Rowan's eyebrows pull together, confused. "I don't care. Either way. It's not— It's not men or women. It's people." Rowan looks to him. "Right now, it's you. Or— It has been you. For a while."

"I'm your manservant," Rowan says, stupidly. He smiles at her, and, Lord above, she would kill for that smile if she had to.

"We all know you're more than that to me," George tells her. There's a long beat of silence.

"You have to tell me your secret," Rowan says, because she needs to know what is going on, despite the fact that a lot is happening right now. George abruptly looks terrified again, no longer smiling, no longer himself.

"It's horrifying," George says. "But you have to believe me."

"I do," Rowan says. "I will."

George starts stripping his clothes off, but he does it so clinically and systematically that Rowan just averts her eyes. She's seen him naked before; she's the one responsible for dressing and undressing him every day. Once his clothes are folded in the corner of the room, he crouches down, gathers up the chains at his feet, and holds them out. "Chain me up."

Rowan stares at him. George shakes the chains, insistent, and she steps forward, still shirtless in her bindings, and takes the chains from him. She unlocks each manacle and snaps them around his wrists and ankles.

"Tighten them," he tells her, and she does, methodically, until he's satisfied. She backs off to the other wall, where she abandoned her shirt. He sits on the ground, so she does, too, curling up with her arms around her bent legs.

"What is it?" she asks, now that he seems satisfied. Moonlight creeps in through the cracks in the ceiling, the stable-floor above them.

"I'm a wolf," he says. Rowan stares at him. "A lycanthrope. Is what I've been told it's called. Lycanthropy."

"Werewolf," Rowan says, softly. "Of course."

"You believe me?" he asks her. Rowan motions at his expression.

"You're being serious," she says, "I can see it on your face. You're not lying." She doesn't know if it's actually possibly true, or if he's just experiencing some sort of mental break, but, either way, he needs her right now. "What happens?"

"For the couple of days a month when the moon is full, at night, I become a wolf," he says. "I can control myself sometimes, but only barely. It's just better that I get locked up down here in case I lose control and hurt someone."

"How did this happen?" Rowan asks, resting her cheek on her knee. At least this makes sense; all the clues are slotting into place. His exhaustion, his monthly disappearances, his sadness, his self-imposed loneliness.

"A creature in the woods," George says. "Years and years ago, when I was only a boy. The bite transforms you." George looks at her, hard. "You shouldn't be here. I could bite you. Or kill you."

"You won't," Rowan says.

"I could."

"So?" Rowan asks. "I'm not gonna leave you alone down here."

George just keeps looking at her.

"I love you," he says. Rowan feels a tear slip down her face, unbidden. "I'm sorry, I shouldn't've said that."

"Say it again when you can do something about it," Rowan tells him. "And when you've thought about it a little. I'm your manservant."

"Be my queen," George says, and Rowan's heart is *pounding* in her chest, but then the moonlight shifts, brightens in their tiny cell. George's eyes blacken, the pupils taking over his irises, then the whites. She watches.

Rowan isn't sure what she thought a werewolf was *supposed* to look like, but George just becomes a wolf. An enormous wolf, but a wolf nonetheless. The shackles stay wrapped around his ankles and wrists as they become a wolf's legs, and he bucks against them. The transformation is grotesque. George's bones crack and snap and fold in on themselves, and the wolf forms from their broken pieces. Rowan knows she will never, ever forget this. She also knows she will never, ever let George go through this alone again.

"Hello," she says, when he's fully transformed into the wolf. George looks up at her with blackened canine eyes and sits down. "Do you understand what I'm saying?" George nods his huge wolf's head. "Can you think?" Another nod. "Can you control yourself?"

George stands again, and the wolf starts to walk over to her. Rowan doesn't move, but the shackles still stop George from reaching her. Once he's at the ends of his chains, he sits down again. She reaches out a hand towards him, and he snaps at her. She yanks her hand back, scooting back across the stones, and he looks... regretful? As sad as a wolf's eyes can be.

"It's okay," Rowan says. She's read books about werewolves. She knows George's brain is supposedly still in there, exactly the same as it is when he *is* a human. She also knows a wolf's instincts are probably impossible to ignore.

Rowan moves carefully forward, a slow crawl back to where George is. He watches her the whole time. By the time she's close enough to touch him, he seems to have settled. She reaches out, slowly, cautiously, so, *so* carefully. He's still, and then she touches the top of his head, and his eyes shut. She pulls herself closer, and he lets her. She rests her head against his chest, feeling the rise and fall of his lungs, and shuts her eyes. It's warm, and comfortable, and it's all she can let herself have, in this terrifying moment.

Her heart is still pounding; she's horrified and afraid. She also knows that if anyone is going to kill her, it may as well be George. If he does just bite her, at least he won't be a werewolf alone. There's some real fear here, but also some resignation, and maybe a little bit of hope. She settles down, and he lifts one of his tremendous legs over her to hold her close. She keeps her eyes closed and falls asleep there.

———————

It's disorienting, waking up on the floor of an underground dungeon cell beneath the king's stables. Rowan can't figure out where she is at first; she assumes maybe she fell asleep on the floor in George's chambers, because she's done that before when she waits too long for him to return and he never does. She feels something warm beside her, underneath her, and she remembers, all at once, the wolf.

She doesn't jump, doesn't stir, because she doesn't want to startle George. Instead, she gingerly lifts her head and looks down. She exhales sharply when she sees the human George sleeping beneath her, still shackled to the floor, instead of the wolf.

George's heavy arm is laid across her, wrapped around her and holding her tight, and she settles back down, pulling him closer to her. He shifts in his sleep, and she hears him yawn, a jaw-cracking thing bringing him closer to wakefulness.

"Ro?" George asks, and Rowan's heart skips ahead, starts racing all over again. "Are you okay?"

Rowan looks herself over. She can see a few scratches across her abdomen, but otherwise, nothing. "I'm okay. Are you?"

George huffs a laugh. He moves to sit up, so Rowan does, too, the two of them inching apart, still sharing space. The air is cold outside of the little bubble of body heat they had created for themselves, and Rowan shifts closer to George without thinking too deeply about it.

"I'm not the one I'm worried about," George says. "You are just so, *so* stupid. You know that, right? You know how stupid you are?"

"It didn't really matter what happened," Rowan tells him. "It's you. I had to do it. I never would've forgiven myself if I left."

George looks her over. "You're insane."

"Maybe," she says.

They're silent for a little while. After a bit, Rowan gets up, goes to George's clothes in the corner, and fishes the key for his shackles out of the pile. She unlocks each manacle and frees him. They both get dressed in near-silence.

"I'm sorry I lied to you," Rowan says, eventually. "I was afraid. But that's not fair. I shouldn't've done it and I understand if you're angry with me."

"I get it," George tells her. He looks away from the doublet in his hands. "I hope you can grow to trust me."

Rowan frowns. "I do trust you."

"Maybe I don't mean trust," George says.

"I stayed with you all night," Rowan reminds him. "When you became a wolf. Do you remember that? Do you remember when I laid down right there and slept through the night with you as a werewolf? Because I think it's pretty clear what I mean by that."

"You talk so much," George tells her. Rowan scoffs. George comes closer to her and lifts his hands, a silent question, and Rowan's pulse accelerates. She nods, and he frames her face in his hands. "I want to court you."

Rowan laughs. "Lord, I wasn't expecting you to say that."

"May I?" George asks. He pauses for a second. "Please?"

"You may," Rowan tells him. He kisses her, lightly, then pulls back. "Would our children be werewolves?"

"Good Lord, please take this one step at a time," George says. "I'm just trying not to turn *you* into a werewolf."

"Maybe it wouldn't be the worst thing in the world," Rowan tells him. She slips out of his hands, gathers up his things, and stuffs them back into his bag, throwing it over her shoulder. George slips the bag off her shoulder and throws it over his own.

"Can't have the object of my affections carrying my things," George says.

"I'm your manservant."

"You're fired."

"See, that's exactly what I was afraid of," Rowan tells him, and George laughs. "Now I don't have a job."

"How does queen sound?" George asks. Rowan bats him away and tugs the rope ladder down off the ceiling.

"See, you keep saying that, but the implications around that are just so enormous I'm having trouble processing it," Rowan tells him. She climbs up the rope ladder, then turns to offer him a hand up as he climbs. They hide the trap door together, then start heading back up towards the castle. "Have you ever had your king reveal that he's a werewolf, tell you that he loves you, and fire you all in twelve hours? Because I have, and let me tell *you*, it's disorienting."

"No, I haven't," George says. "It is a limitation of mine, I'll admit. Should I try it? Have you enjoyed it?"

"No," Rowan says, forcefully, and George laughs.

"My manservant is a woman who I'm madly in love with," George reminds her. "Isn't that enough of a shock?"

"I really don't think they compare," Rowan tells him, drily. By the time they reach the castle, Rowan is shivering. George shrugs his fur cloak off and puts it over her shoulders. "You don't want to have to explain—"

"Maybe I do," George says. "Maybe I should tell everyone. I am *officially* pursuing my manservant, and she's going to give me an heir, too."

"George—"

"Oh, sweet music," George says, grinning, and Rowan buries her face in her hands. "My name is music in your voice—"

"I *despise* you—"

"Maybe I should change our coat of arms to have a wolf," George muses, as he leads Rowan through the castle to the kitchens. "Would this be too obvious? Of course, I could slip it through the cracks while I tell everyone I'm courting my manservant. That ought to be distraction enough."

"You're a madman," Rowan tells him, but she's really just happy he's back to his usual self. *This* is the man she loves, not the frightened man of the night before. She stops in her tracks, and he stops a couple of steps ahead of her, turning back to raise an eyebrow at her. "I love you."

George grins at her. "I've done what you've asked, and I thought about it, and I love you, too." George backtracks to her, offers her his arm, and she takes it. He resumes escorting her to the kitchens. "Even as a wolf, you were all I could think about."

"You'd think you would have more pressing concerns," Rowan comments, but George just shakes his head. She's joking, but he's not, for once.

"Not when it comes to you," George says. "Not now." He shoves open the door to the kitchens and sweeps her in. "Now, eat something, you pretty thing. My queen won't starve on my watch."

"Stop calling me that," Rowan tells him.

"But you've already applied and I find you suitable for the position," George replies. She flings a hunk of bread at him, and he catches it between his teeth. He chews and swallows, then says, smiling, "Your references are *phenomenal*. You were the manservant to the king? Do tell. Also, should I call your father about a dowry?"

"Not unless you want some corn and a sheep," Rowan says, digging up some cheese to go with their bread.

"I could go for some corn," George says. He sits and pats his thigh, and Rowan goes to him, red-faced, and climbs into his lap. He buries his face in the juncture of her neck and shoulder and sighs. "I could get used to this. I *will* get used to this."

"You're a werewolf," Rowan says, suddenly, and he laughs.

"Absolutely," he tells her. "Absolutely I am."

ABOUT THE AUTHOR

Nicole Mello is a fiction author who has been writing since before her memory was a functional thing. She has three published works: *Venus* (2017), *The Modern Prometheus* (2018), and the book in your hands right now (2018). She has her B.A. in Creative Writing from Lesley University. She currently resides in Boston, Massachusetts with her partner and two best friends. She daylights as a museum educator and loves to talk about history, space, movies, dogs, cryptids, true crime, and human rights.

She wants to remind you to keep being yourself.

Question everything. Stay hydrated.

11972097R00248

Made in the USA
Lexington, KY
17 October 2018